THE
KRAKEN

by Don C. Reed

Boyds Mills Press

Text copyright © 1995 by Don C. Reed
Jacket illustration copyright © by Boyds Mills Press

Published by Caroline House
Boyds Mills Press, Inc.
A Highlights Company
815 Church Street
Honesdale, Pennsylvania 18431
Printed in the United States of America

Publisher Cataloging-in-Publication Data
Reed, Don C.
    The kraken / by Don C. Reed.—1st ed.
[224]p. : cm.
Includes bibliography.
Summary : A young boy confronts a giant squid off the coast of Newfoundland in
this adventure set in a nineteenth-century fishing village.
ISBN 1-56397-216-6
1. Newfoundland—History—Juvenile fiction. 2. Sea stories—Juvenile literature.
[1. Newfoundland—History—Fiction. 2. Sea stories.] I. Title.
813'.54 [F]—dc20   1995   CIP
Library of Congress Catalog Card Number 93-74140

First edition, 1995
Book designed by Tim Gillner
The text of this book is set in 11.5-point New Baskerville.
Distributed by St. Martin's Press

10 9 8 7 6 5 4 3 2 1

◆ ◆ ◆

AUTHOR'S NOTE

While visiting Portugal Cove, Newfoundland, I met the great-great-great-great-grandnephew of Tom Piccot. Mark was only ten years old that summer, but he was agile, alert, and well-muscled for his age. It was surprisingly easy to imagine him in perilous battle with a giant squid, as his ancestor had done. A cocky little kid he was—bouncy, full of energy—and the first thing he said to me, in that unmistakable Newfoundland accent, was:

"Well, 'ood you be dedicatin' your book to, now?"

I told him I had not decided yet, and did he have any suggestions?

"'Ow about the Piccos* of Portugal Cove, then?" he said.

And so it is.

TO THE PICCOS AND PICCOTS OF PORTUGAL COVE AND ALL WHO WORK UPON THE SEA this book is happily dedicated.

Since almost no one could read and write well in nineteenth-century Newfoundland, spellings of names went mainly by sound. Over the years, the letter "t" in Piccot was sometimes dropped, and sometimes not.

And (if you are interested) Newfoundland is pronounced Newf-n-land with the accent on the last syllable.

◆ ◆ ◆

◆ ◆ ◆

ACKNOWLEDGMENTS

I would like to thank

John Maunder, curator of biology at the Newfoundland Museum, for giving an afternoon of his time to a stranger, and especially for unpacking the preserved carcass of a thirty-two-foot giant squid ("just a little one," he apologized!) so I could take a good look at it;

the descendants of the original Tom Piccot, who fought the living monster on the waters of Portugal Cove, October 26, 1873, especially family historian Neil, who showed me the ruins of Tom's old house, pointed out the place in the water where the giant squid rose, and also introduced me to Mark, Lisa, and Michael, the great-great-great-great-grandniece and nephews of Tom;

Paulette Kinnaird, owner of the Red Lion Lodge (originally Tom's combination church and school) in Portugal Cove, who took my wife, Jeannie, barehand-fishing for capelin;

Margueritte Ahldrich, widow of giant-squid expert Fred Ahldrich and herself the author of such papers as "Teuthoid Radulas (the rough-edged "tongue") in Squid," for allowing me to visit and "talk squid";

Newfoundland fishermen Alvah Lee, who showed me how to "face" a cod, removing the facial cartilage for frying; ninety-two-year-old George Churchill, who took me on "a dodge along the landwash" and who walks again in these pages; and especially Bill Day's son Alex, who drove me around Tom Piccot's old stomping grounds so I could "get it right about the lay of the land";

◆ ◆ ◆

Newfoundland researchers Deborah Snow, A. C. Randall, and John Gerard McRae, as well as stateside friend Teresa Troutman;

Newfoundland book publishers Jesperson Press, Breakwater Books, Harry Cuff & Sons, and Dicks & Co., without whose help this book would not have been possible;

Frank W. Lane, whose classic book *Kingdom of the Octopus* first introduced me to Tom Piccot and the giant squid;

Farley Mowat (familiar to American readers as the author of *Never Cry Wolf*), whose book *Newfoundland: This Rock Within the Sea* excited me to find out more about the amazing fisherfolk country;

and incredible author Judith Ross Enderle, who helped in ways only another writer and editor (she is both) can fully understand. To name one instance alone, this book was originally a forty-three-page epic poem! Fortunately, Ms. Enderle was able to suggest a better way.

THE
KRAKEN

CHAPTER ONE

ON THE WATER IN THE NIGHT

◆　◆　◆

October 19, 1872

As Tom Piccot stepped out in the Newfoundland night, he heard a noise that didn't fit—a rasping sound, with grunts intermixed, as if some great animal were breathing hard and sharpening its claws. Then it stopped.

For a moment Tom considered going back into the warmth and light of the kitchen. Maybe he should ask Skipper Theo to come out. His father would know what that sound had been.

But then Tom remembered his big sister, Lynny, and how she loved to tease. He could just hear her: "Feared of the dark, are ya, b'y? Too young to row out on the sea by yerself?" He shut the door firmly, settling it into place with a creak of leather hinges. He was almost twelve years old, practically a man, and a fisherman since he was six.

The winds swirled. He shivered all over violently, just the once. He felt the cold keenly, even through his yellow oil-skin jacket and pants, his father's patched workshirt, a silver wool sweater Ma had made for him, another pair of pants, and long underwear. After that one "wake-up" shake, he accepted the chill instead of wasting energy trying to hide from it.

He knew he should get moving. But still he hesitated on the bare ground just outside the door.

From where he stood, halfway up Grayman's Beard Hill, Tom could see most of the small fishing village around the half-circle of shoreline. Some shadows on the hill were houses, earth-colored like his, brown from a homemade crude paint of red earth, seawater, and cod-liver oil that took a year to dry and was not really safe to lean against even then. He saw the cove opening to the Atlantic. The waves tonight glowed pale blue-green where they frothed on the shore. And the docks, called fishing stages, reached out like long arms to the sea.

Hard as he could, Tom listened for that one strange sound. He heard the hiss of waves rushing in along the landwash, and the grinding rumble of rocks tumbling over one another in the surge; heard the creak of wooden piers, and the groan of dock ropes stretching as the boats they held rose and fell. He heard the burbling trickle of the brook winding down the hills to Portugal Cove.

Behind him! The noise came again, and Tom spun around, looking up the side of the hill to that outcropping of granite boulders called "The Lookout."

It was Noddy Weathers, out hanging his dog.

Or, rather, trying to. The animal was a Newfoundland, looking big as a half-grown bear. In the moonlight Tom could barely see the rope indenting the hairy neck, as the

man and dog wrestled on the edge of The Lookout—
Noddy Weathers shoving hard, the dog bracing his legs,
showing very little interest in being hanged.

"Hey, Uncle," called Tom, for the man was of the same
village as he, though no actual relation.

"Hey, b'y," answered the man shortly. Another long
moment of grunting and scuffle and that scratch of blunt
claws against rock. Then Noddy Weathers paused to
breathe.

"What's to do?" asked Tom, running lightly up the goat
path.

"This piece o' rubbish won't do no work! I puts he in
harness for to pull wood, and natural I hits him a time or
two wi' a stick on the head t' educate him. But soon as I
hits him, will he tug the slide? He will not! An' the harder
I hits him, the less he'll do. Now he won't mind me at all.
Stubborn or lazy, I can't tell the which. And I traded a
dozen good fishhooks fer him to a Micmac passin'
through! That Indian got the best o' me fer sure. Fool dog
just sits there smilin', and he so big t' others feared to make
him mind.

"I can't feed no dog won't work! Can't turn him loose
neither. He'd starve, which ain't no blessing; or eat my
goats, which is worse. You know I can't afford wastin' powder and shot to kill no dog; he's too big and troublesome
to drown, nor he won't hold still fer the ax. So I'll be after
hangin' him."

Tom squatted. The huge young dog panted, breath
steaming from its jaws as it looked up at him. A long pink
tongue shot out and licked Tom's face. Tom wiped his
cheek and drew back a little. "Slobberin' creature—how
old he be?"

"Don't know. Too old to learn, I expect. But look at the

size o' he! All them muscles? Could pull a slide by hisself. Niver seen no dog big as that, nor one eats more. Hmmph, nor lazier!" Noddy spat.

"Got webbed toes," observed Tom, lifting and spreading one large hairy paw.

"Oh, he's a water dog, sure enough, but prob'ly too lazy to swim!"

"What do ya call him?"

"Hmmph! Curses mostly! That's what I calls him! That dog have got hisself a attytude problem!"

Tom laughed. "Attytude! That's what old Teacher Treadwell always said about me last year. 'Tom, you got yer-self a attytude problem,' he'd say, and start whompin' on me."

Noddy Weathers sighed. He was not a mean man. He adjusted one end of the rope around his waist and snugged the noose tighter on the dog's neck. He edged his boots under the huge hairy body, ready to shove it over the edge.

"Let me take him, Uncle," said Tom quickly.

"Take him? What fer?"

"Don't know—play toy, p'rhaps."

"What'll yer ma say to that, you wantin' to feed this great, worthless creature?"

Tom groaned. "I don't know. Maybe if we does good at settlin' up when the merchant comes, we'll have a bit extra food fer the year. I do need me a dog, though. Can I trade ya somethin' fer 'im? 'Course I can't give ya no fishhooks, but then you admits he ain't worth that much."

The man snorted. "Ah, well, bring me a fish, clean and coarse-salted, mind—just the next one ya catches, don't be takin' none o' the good stuff from yer family's pile. An' here, I'll throw in the rope to hang 'im with. You'll be needin' it, I thinks."

"Next fish I catches," Tom promised. Rope, dog, and problem passed into his hands.

Noddy Weathers went down the winding goat path, and Tom studied what he had just bought. "Well, I couldn't let him hang you, could I?" he said, running his fingers through the coal-black mane. Warmth spread out from the dog's great body. He already weighed more than his master's 110 pounds. He would eat a lot, for sure. Tom held the dog's head still and looked squarely into the small red-brown eyes.

"Pay attention now, dog. Uncle Noddy, he told you straight. We all lives close to the bone here. We has to work, or we don't eat. I mean, folks sez *I'm* lazy, and I don't niver stop slavin'! Well, hardly niver anyway.

"But see, only people got money is the merchants, and they don't care if we lives or dies. They sells us supplies and buys our fish, robbin' us at both ends—and that's if we has the fish to sell. Lately nobody's catchin' much.

"Last year in the starvin' time, March and April, when the stored food give out and the new fish was'n' come, three people died. Uncle Noddy there? He lost his littlest boy, Samivel, just four years old. The hunger made him weak; he took sick and died. And him no older than—" Tom remembered Baby Sally at home, how little she looked in her white flannel nightgown and swansdown leggings. Not to mention Mark Josephus, who was six. Tom stood up abruptly. Best not think about it.

"Well, I got to catch me some crawler. You come along. Try and stay outta the way." He tugged the rope, but the big dog was already on his feet.

As Tom walked, he began to plan his arguments for Ma. His father would be no trouble. Skipper Theo never said much about anything except, of course, the merchants (he always had something to say about them!) and fish and weather and such as that. But Ma, well . . . He'd figure out something.

He stopped.

"I know what I'll call ya," he said, nodding. "Yis, b'y, I'm gonna call ya Murphy. After poor cousin Murphy what drowned in the big wind in '68."

Murphy voiced no objection, and was named.

"This is me dory," said Tom as they arrived at the shore. "Ain't she grand?"

The black boat rested at the top of the slipway: a series of half-buried logs, their rounded sides acting like rollers easing entry to the sea.

"I made her meself, every inch, hardly no help from Skipper nor Grandfather, 'cept useless ad-vice. I cut the trees, sawed the boards, tied and steamed and bent 'em. And looky there, that little round bulge underneath the tar? That ain't no wooden peg, me son. This boat's got near ten dozen nails in her, real iron, flattened on the inside end. I clinted them nails meself, see? Poundin' in from one side whilst I held my tom-hawk sideways 'gainst t' other. That way your nailhead, she swells up, won't pull out. After that I took tarred twine and pounded it into her seams, and then tarred she all over, stem to starn, ever'thin' 'cept the thwart where I sits, 'cause I don't want to sit on no tarry board, 'specially when it gets hot."

Murphy walked back and forth as if eager to get going, but Tom was too proud to stop short.

"Snug, you say? This boat don't know what leakin' is. And steady? You could dance in her.

"Her name," he said, lowering his voice and looking around, "is the *R.M.C.* I tells most folks that stands fer

Royal Marine Corps. But what it really means is Rosie May Crandall. On account of I got a friend, special, and that's her name."

The moonlight laid a bright gold path across the waves.

Bragging done, Tom grabbed and heaved until the small boat moved down the slipway logs. The twelve-foot dory weighed three hundred pounds, but the logs were well blubbered with fat from a leopard seal caught three days ago in the Andersons' nets. Tom was sturdy and strong, but not tall. He did not know his actual height, never having been measured except with a piece of string when clothes had to be sewed. But once when Lynny told him he was really kind of short, Tom said no, he wasn't short, just built close to the ground!

As the boat came awash in the surf, Murphy leaped into the stern.

"Oh, ya knows about boats, does ya? Well, see can ya catch us some crawler tonight. We'll be needin' the bait if we finds any cod later on."

Tom waded out another couple steps, then hopped aboard. His boat glided, then rose over a low foaming swell. He picked up the oars.

"I hear some of them St. John's fellers eats crawler by its ownself. Calls it lobster, they do." He shook his head. "Imagine that, eatin' somethin' crawls on the seafloor like a bug? Disgustin'.

"'Course," he added, spitting over the side, "them St. John's fellers'll do anythin'. Merchants mostly, and crazy mean. They puts gold more important than people."

The black boat slid smoothly over the waves. Oars creaked between tholepins tied there by thin cedar roots as flexible as string. The Newfoundland winds, never far away, *shushed* and *whoo-oo-ooshed* around them as Tom rowed and rowed, and was not lost.

To locate himself on the water, Tom used high points on the land. He lined up the three churches: Catholic to the west, around the bend from Sail Point; Salvation Army to the east; Church of England in the middle. The Church of England also functioned as a school, which Tom unhappily attended, and also was the lodge on those rare occasions when strangers visited. But there were few visitors. Portugal Cove was not a big port; not like St. John's, the capital of Newfoundland, with thousands of people bumping elbows. Portugal Cove was a sleepy little outport—or at least it looked sleepy to outsiders. To the *liveyers*, those who "lived here," Portugal Cove was everything a person could sensibly want.

The *Rosie May* moved past the little unnamed island the Piccots claimed—a tiny thing not more than ten yards across, connected to the land by a long wooden footbridge. A casual glance did not reveal its value, this fishing place so near the shore. But the seafloor went deep right before it, a narrow canyon leading to the sea. The pattern of waves and currents was such that most fish swimming into Portugal Cove came right between the island and the shore. It was the very best place to net cod in the cove. When, of course, there were fish to catch.

But Tom was after crawler tonight. Maybe some handlining after; get Murphy's fish for Uncle Noddy and a couple to bring home for fresh. Maybe even one for the teacher; get on his good side for once.

School, he remembered glumly. Soon.

Oh, please, Tom prayed silently, don't let fat old Whipper Treadwell come back! So stuck up 'cause he's related to the merchant, him and that phony English accent—"My nephew attends school in England"—

whoopdeedoo. Him all the time beatin' on kids, and proud of it. "You can tell a Treadwell student," Tom had once heard the schoolmaster brag, "by the purple of their hands." He used a doubled leather strap, which he called "the cane," and whipped the kids' hands black and blue if they did not know the answers. Generally the left hand was struck; the right considered more needful for work.

Tom tightened the fingers of his left hand around the oar, remembering.

He could not wait to quit school. This year or next, he'd find a way. The two years' schooling he already had, that was plenty. What did he need with books anyway? He was a fisherman!

"Well, here we go, b'y," he said, "this is where the first trap goes."

Tom's trap was a flat plate of tarred metal with four holes. The middle hole was for bait. Rope went through the three outer holes and knotted underneath, and a short piece of net wove around the side ropes. Once lowered to the seafloor, the net walls collapsed. On a lucky night, the lobster would crawl over them and be caught when you pulled up the trap.

The bait was a cod head, a pile of which he had picked up several days earlier and set on board. They had aged nicely, so rotten they glowed like blue-white ghost heads in the night. Stink? Whew!

He tossed the baited trap over the side. Fishing twine slid through his fingers. When a bump and some slack let him know the trap had landed, Tom tied on a marker buoy near the end of the premeasured line, tossed that over, too. Had to be able to find it later on.

As his boat neared the next spot for crawler, Tom looked back to shore. Each family, if they had a fisherman out or not, put a seal-oil lamp in the window. He found the light that belonged to his house and felt warmed by it. Going after crawler was easy, especially with such a small line of traps. Even so, it was dark on the face of the sea.

Crawler were best caught at night, when they hunted. During the day they snoozed, and it was rare to see the big-clawed crustaceans with their lightfooted crawl or quick scoot across the seafloor.

The second trap went down, and the third.

At each splash of the dory's oars, a blue-green light shone briefly on the water, leaving pale tracks on the sea. The eerie glow was sea fire, some tiny animal's cold light, and it didn't worry Tom much. Grandfather said sea fire meant a storm was on the way, but then a storm was always on the way in Newfoundland. The game was to guess how long you had before it arrived. Tom sniffed the air, listened to the winds, and scanned the sky from beach to horizon. He had time.

Over the side the fourth pot went. Way down deep he saw a green stir of movement as some great fish shot by, igniting a track of living light. Was it after something? Or trying to get away? No way to tell for sure.

Four crawler pots, that was all. Hardly worth doing, Tom thought. He had been after his father to let him do more, but Grandfather opposed it. "A boy needs his beauty sleep, he do," Grandfather would say, and Tom would always answer, "Hey, I'm too pertty now, all the girls is after me!" But in truth there was only one girl he cared for, and he never talked about her.

Tom sighed. He wished Grandfather would hurry and get well. It wasn't good how Old Skipper looked, kind of yellowy and weak.

"Well, let's see what we got, Murphy, me b'y." They were

back at the first pot. Tom reached out with the gaff, hauling up buoy and line, then coiling it neatly behind him.

Nothing. Even the fish-head bait was gone.

"Well, skunked on that one."

The second and third traps were empty as well.

But the fourth pot held a whole lobster and a small dark fragment beside it. Tom grabbed the crawler quick by the back, just behind the claws, holding it tight.

But there was no movement. The crawler felt wrong. Way too light.

He lifted the dead thing closer to him. He found a narrow break on the shell's back and wiggled a finger inside it. The crawler was . . . empty. A hole in the back and the insides all gone. Had someone caught and opened it, plucked out the insides before putting it back in his trap? Was somebody playing a joke? He listened for laughter, yelled out, "You there, Jimmy Anderson, you snot-nosed sleeveen?" But no sound came back except the song of the sea and the whisper of the wind.

Tossing the shell overside, Tom reached for the other object. It was a lobster claw, the meat still fresh inside. Something had poached his trap.

He pitched the claw over, too, then studied the moon and the dark clouds forming.

"I think we've still got time. Sure don't want to go back empty," he said. "Maybe we can snag a skinny fish for Uncle Noddy to pay yer price." It seemed so natural to talk with Murphy as he sprawled across the stern thwart.

A half-hour's row took him to Oar's Deep, a favorite spot, where Tom believed he could always catch at least a couple fish, maybe some big logy lunkers, the ones that swam alone.

Needing time for the hook-and-line fishing, Tom tossed

the homemade anchor over the side. The wood-and-stone kellick would keep them from drifting. Move six feet away from a chosen spot and the bottom conditions could change altogether; a difference in underwater neighborhoods could mean you caught no fish.

He rigged handlines and stood, feeling the ripple of the water through his boots and the boat.

Two lead-weighted hooks plopped in the water, one on each side of the boat. Tom was jigging, and the only bait was a fish-shaped chunk of lead with three hooks, one for each line. When he felt the thud of bottom-finding, he pulled the jigger up a couple feet and began to twitch the lines, one in each hand, back and forth across his chest, left hand and right. He hoped to foul-hook a fish, snag it with the lead-weight jig.

Most of the cod had moved back from the shore, but there were still a few of the green-and-gold-backed fish lurking about. They would be the bigger ones, the kind that would not need to school with others for safety. Earlier in the season the cod were too full of easy-caught capelin to fall for the trick, but now those little fish were gone, and maybe . . .

A tug.

Murphy crouched.

Tom yanked, feeling the snag of impact. Instantly he was hauling up—a fish, big one, two-foot-long cod, but not well-hooked. Cod don't fight much, but even so it was going to get loose. Right at the surface he saw the hook come out of its lip. Too late for the boathook.

"Argh!" Tom said. Then Murphy jumped overboard.

Tom was astonished as dog and fish disappeared, but when Murphy bobbed up, the fish was in his mouth. The big dog dropped the flopping cod into the boat, and Tom helped his new partner scramble aboard. Murphy made no motion to eat the fish and sat upright in the stern, breathing lightly, tongue out. His hair shone wet in the moonlight.

"Yer a *fishin'* dog!" said Tom. "I skunked Noddy Weathers fer sure! Wait'll I tell—"

From the left side of the boat came a stronger tug, like lightning flashing up the line. This was no weak-fighting cod. The pull almost yanked him in. Even through clothes he felt the line burn a welt across his wrist and forearm.

"Halibut!"

Some folks did not like halibut, a fish that fought long and had many bones. The food's not worth the fight, those people said.

But Tom never liked to let any catch go. In a quick swirl of movement he warped the twine across his jacket back, spreading out the line of pain. He wished he had his nipper gloves to ease the strain on his hands, but they were out of reach in the boat's forward cuddy.

The dory jerked back and forth, and Tom rocked with it.

They fought. The halibut was a great flat fish, wonderfully strong.

Tom's legs and back ached. Sweat ran in his eyes. His breath grew hot and short, but he took line when he could and eased off when he must.

An hour passed before the fighting weight began to rise.

Careful, Tom told himself. When it gets near, chop its head with the tom-hawk. Don't let it come overside with any life left; might bust a thwart, even flip the dory. He located the hand ax with his foot, fumbled it near.

Up and up he dragged the halibut. He saw the pale flash of belly as it turned and twisted just ten feet below the

Rosie May's hull. He could see it all now, clear in the moonlight and glowing water. Hundred pounds, maybe more. That was a whole bunch of food, even supposing the bones.

Maybe he would give it to Noddy Weathers, too, make him happy about the trade, and—

Something *else* was rising, underneath the halibut. Something so huge a bulge of water came before it, swelling the surface as if a great whale was rising.

It's just a school of herring, Tom told himself, whole bunch of 'em, that's why it looks so big. He waited for the school to change direction.

But it was not many fish; it was only one creature.

And it did not turn away.

WHAT SANK THE SCHOONER PEARL

◆　◆　◆

T he fishline went forgotten. Tom froze.

Looking bigger and bigger as it neared, the creature below him changed colors: now white, now purplish pink, finally a hue unrecognizable in the dark, but which Tom knew was deepest red, the color of blood and of rage. For he had seen this beast before in smaller version a thousand times.

It was . . . a squid, a giant squid, five times the length of his boat. The eyes were huge, black and dead-white, and flickering a hideous green.

The body was shaped like a spear: the blade pointed back toward the deeps it was leaving; the arms at the front came together, streamlined for speed until the instant came for attack.

As now. Enormous, long arms lashed out, two of them, the hunting tentacles: reaching ropy thongs with ends like fingerless "hands," and each hand bigger than Tom. These clutched the exhausted halibut. Now the shorter, thicker arms flared out and picked and touched as, spiderlike, the beast attached itself to the fish—*Tom's* fish. Even through his fear Tom felt a dull red glimmer of resentment.

The halibut went stiff, as if it had been bitten, then trembled and partly disappeared beneath the web of flesh at the base of the giant squid's arms.

All seemed sinuous motion: the many arms clever as fingers, plucking bits and pieces of the halibut; and fast as they were torn away the pieces slid somehow *along* the arms, conveyed toward the central mass and the dark beak Tom knew was there. And the eyes, those monstrous eyes changing color—now midnight black, now vivid green—so strange and yet somehow familiar. How long before those cold, unblinking orbs should turn upward and see him?

Tom wanted to move, but his muscles would not obey. He could only stand and stare in fixed fascination as the creature fed.

Then came the most tremendous noise from something warm and huge by his side, between him and the thing in the water.

The dog he had named Murphy *roared*.

As if from a dream Tom shook himself. He pitched the fishline off his shoulders and dived for the oars. When he sat down to row, he missed the seat. Instead he sat on something cold and soft that moved! He scrambled up, but it was only the cod he had caught earlier, now somewhat flattened.

Then Tom was back on the thwart, hustling, frantic to get away. His first oar stroke missed the water on the right, so the boat turned a half-circle. He got the oars together and leaned hard again, heaving with the strength of desperation. The blades bit and dug—getaway getaway getaway—NO, it had him, the boat yanked back! The anchor! Tom dropped the oars, snatched the bait ax, chopped the rope. Then he saw two coils of fishline. The hook was still in the halibut. He was fastened to the monster! But which coil held it? He pitched both overside and grabbed the oars again.

He rowed as he had never rowed before, muscles heaving. He felt like a bug on a pond with a great fish underneath. Any instant it could turn and rise.

Rain began, a pecking drizzle first, then scattered patterns like cats' paws, imprinted on the waves. The wind shifted, eddying for a moment, then seemed to make up its mind and increased steadily. The rain also became stronger and more constant, closing in Tom's field of vision.

Murphy settled in the stern. Rain didn't bother a Newfoundland dog. He might not be wearing yellow oilskins, but his double-layered hair with undercoat insulation kept him always ready for damp weather.

Tom rowed until the frenzy left him, and then he kept on rowing. With the rain blocking out his visual landmarks, he had to trust his sense of direction to bring him safely home.

As he came nearer shore he could see again, and he adjusted his course, avoiding the anchored boats. He rowed until the dory bumped, ramming halfway up on the slipway, his peeled-log exit from the sea.

"Ahhh!" Tom said.

Twisting his wrists so that the oars fell inboard, he floundered over, splashing, then hauled his boat out of reach of the rising tide. He wanted to run home to warmth, shelter, family.

But he stopped and stood for a moment in the rain, trying to still his trembling legs.

"The fish," he said to the big dog beside him. "I've got to take care of me fish." When he said fish he meant cod, just cod, and nothing else. Other fish species were called by their names, but the green-and-brown cod with its two chin "whiskers" was so important that it was just "the fish," and every Newfoundlander knew exactly what you meant.

Hauling the heavy cod by the gill slits, Tom hurried up the sloping beach.

At the end of a long-legged pier was a low-roofed building: the fisherman's store. Nothing was sold here; it was where they stored things.

He hoped someone would be working, yet no one was there. But the crude lamp—just a flickering bowl of slow-burning cod livers—was lit, its smoky yellow flame lending weird illumination so that Tom's shadow danced grotesquely on the wall.

Dumping his fish on the table, Tom reached to where the throat-cutter was, and with that thin, sharp blade made two incisions—slash and slash—one on each side of the fish's neck just behind the gill slit. A cut underneath opened jawline to vent, and his fingers fumbled in the body cavity, finding the liver by its shape. He tossed that quickly to the rot pot, where time, sun, and decay would release the precious cod-liver oil. The rest of the insides he scooped out and dumped down the trunk hole in the floor, below which the ocean moved slowly, softly, as if sneaking up.

Then, sliding the body of the cod so the head was just over the edge of the table, Tom leaned down hard with his left hand. *Snap!* the backbone broke. With a yank of his other hand he pulled the fish's body away from the head. The fish skull fell. He foot-swept it into the trunk hole. There was a splitter's knife somewhere for what came next, but he didn't see it handy and didn't feel like hunting for it. The throat-cutter blade worked almost as well. He split the fish longways. The headless, gutted cod opened up like a book.

Three steps to the right was a waist-high box, which Tom unlidded quickly. Removing a handful of large-grained salt, he rubbed it into the flesh of the cod.

The fish was now coarse-salted. At the trunk hole Tom hauled a bucket of chill seawater to wash his hands, then leaned over and threw up.

Which last relieved him considerably.

"There goes me supper," Tom said to Murphy. "Oh, well, the skulpins'll eat good fer oncet." The bony-faced fish living under the dock served as garbage disposals, gulping anything remotely edible.

Tom set the fish on top of Noddy Weathers's pile. The new fish would be recognized, different from the ones underneath; each fisherman had his own methods, and the knife work could be told apart. Uncle Noddy's cut fish were sure easy to spot. He had arthritis in his hands, which made his splitting work ragged.

Tom glanced at his family's uneven store of half-dried fish "in waterhorse," called so because the shape of the pile faintly resembled a waterhorse, or hippopotamus, that one fisherman had seen on a long-ago trip to Africa. Tomorrow, if weather permitted, they would set the fish out again to dry in the last pale rays of October sun.

When the fish was "made"—hard-dried, salted, and fully air-cured—Tom, his father, and their shareman, Daniel

Squires, would carry it up to the family twine loft. There the dry fish would be divided into four-foot stacks, each weighing 112 pounds, dry weight. This was one quintal. So far they had 120 quintals of dried fish. In a good year they might have made 300. But this had not been a good year.

As he gave the one fish onto Noddy Weathers's pile, Tom had a faint uneasy feeling, as if maybe he was stealing from his family. To trade away even one fish was a matter of importance when there was danger of people starving to death. But a deal was a deal.

Tom walked out into the moonlight, then headed up the path to home.

"You can sleep under the house," he said to Murphy, who followed quietly. The rope dragged behind him, forgotten by both. Murphy had slept outdoors all his life. He would survive.

Aching for warmth and comfort, Tom was glad to look up and see his house halfway up on Grayman's Beard Hill—but why were so many windows glowing? Every lamp they owned must be lit. House looked on fire, it was so bright.

Something was wrong. Ma always left one lamp in the window so he could see it from a distance, know that he was thought of—but not like this.

Tom opened the gate of the low riddley fence. Thin branches with the bark peeled off wove around posts driven in the ground—the fence kept the neighbor's goats away from their garden.

"You mess with the goats, I can't save you," Tom said.

The back of the house rested on sloping bedrock; the front was held up by thick beams, with an open basement underneath. Tom crawled in, feeling the cold rock rough on his palms. There was a stack of smooth boards, and he spread these out for the dog. There were piles of net, and these he moved around, making a corner, trying to block out some wind. He reached up, touching the floor of the house.

"This is where the kitchen is," he said. "The warmest spot." Murphy's heavy coat brushed up against Tom. He patted Murphy a minute, remembered how the dog had stood on the boat between him and the danger. "You'm my dog now," he said. "In the mornin', I'll bring ya some of me breakfast."

Murphy settled down, and Tom pulled another pile of net in close, leaving a narrow opening in case the dog had to go out and do his nuisance.

Then Tom backed out, puzzled again by the brightly-lit house. What was going on?

As he pulled back the door on its stiff leather hinges, he saw that the kitchen was jammed full of women, like the times they were planning a social or organizing food for the schoolmaster—but so late? It didn't make sense.

Then Rosie stepped up, hands in the pockets of her long work dress.

Rosie. Large, dark brown eyes and her hair also brown but sheened with red, shimmering in the firelight. Taller than Tom, Rosie was slender and tough as a young willow tree. Lately she had become much embarrassed by her hands, which were large and chapped by work. She was always hiding them in her pockets or behind her. Tom thought she was the most beautiful girl in the world. He waited for her smile. But tonight she did not smile. The light behind her eyes only flickered in recognition of him, then she looked down.

"Tom," she said, as if he had suddenly become a problem.

"What's to do, Rosie?" he said softly, and wondered why

it was so difficult to talk to her. Last year when he was eleven, they had been friends, like two boys together; but this year, well, things were different somehow. Changing.

She looked back at him, straight. Their eyes locked. Tom felt warmer, from the kitchen stove, no doubt.

She spoke and everything changed, as if the floor had shaken under his feet.

"Yer *grandfather's* asking fer you, Tom. Says he wants to give you his blessing."

He wants to give me his blessing? That was what people said of somebody about to die. This must be some mistake, a part of the nightmare begun on the sea.

Tom ran past Rosie. The thump of his boots echoed on the stairs, then he was turning the corner at the top. The door to Grandfather's room stood open, the lamplight flickering within. It was the warmest room in the house, just over the kitchen.

Crowded inside, silent men pulled back, opening a path to Grandfather's bed. He lay there, talking slowly to the tall, bearded fisherman who held his hand.

"'Tis been a pleasure, Will," said Grandfather.

The bearded man could only agree, "Yis, b'y, it have been that."

How odd, Tom thought numbly, that a younger man would call an older man a boy. Grandfather was old, so old. The neighbor gently lowered Grandfather's hand to the white comforter. The skin on the back of his hand looked thin, showing blue veins, not seeming strong enough to hold all the scars and the knobbly bones within.

Baby Sally and Mark Josephus stood by together, having already been blessed.

"Grandfather?" said Tom, lifting the frail, old hand between his two young, strong ones.

"There ya be." Grandfather turned his head slowly. Tom feared he might look weird now. But the blue, blue eyes were still the same, like windows open to the sky. Tom leaned down and hugged him.

"I was out fishin'," he said, straightening up.

"Nay," said Grandfather in pretended surprise. "I thought ya was out pullin' flowers."

"P'rhaps fer another flower, like—a Rose?" said Daniel Squires, their neighbor and shareman, who loved any chance for a laugh.

"No such of a thing!" said Tom, feeling his ears turn red.

Then he remembered and quickly changed the subject. "Grandfather!" he said, "I saw the devil! It took me halibut!"

"What do ya want wi' a halibut? Only good to rip nets." Tom realized his father, Theo, was standing beside him.

"What did ya see?" prompted Daniel Squires, always ready for a story.

"Well, it—" Tom stopped, trying to put words to what he'd seen. "It was like . . . a squid, only big, bigger'n me boat, bigger'n a house, big as any whale." He waited for the room to explode in laughter.

They had all caught squid for bait. Everyone knew what the many-armed creatures were, twelve to eighteen inches long. Nothing that small could steal a man's fish.

But nobody laughed or said anything, not right away.

"It took me halibut," Tom said to fill the silence.

"No loss there," said Daniel Squires. "Halibut ain't worth the trouble nohow." A ripple of agreement went through the men.

"Did ya lose the line?" asked his father.

"Yis," said Tom, not feeling it necessary to mention that he had in fact lost *two* lines, and the anchor rope as well.

Another kellick could be easily made. But rope? That was dear.

"Don't be blamin' the boy, Theophilous," said Grandfather. He usually stuck up for Tom.

"I seen you out the window," said Daniel Squires quickly, before Theo had time to get angry. "Was that a bear walkin' behind o' ya?"

"No, that's me new dog, Murphy, named after me cousin what died in the Big Wind, '68. I traded Noddy Weathers a fish fer 'im."

"Your ma won't feed no dogs," said Theophilous Piccot.

"Dogfish," said Grandfather.

Lately Grandfather's mind took strange jumps, and it was not always easy to see where he was going, nor where from.

"No, Skipper," said Theophilous, and Tom was surprised at the gentleness in his father's voice. "We ain't talkin' about no net-robbin' dogfish, them miserable, worthless excuses fer a shark. This is just some dog Tom wants to keep, and ya knows his ma can't abide no dogs."

"Dog*fish*," repeated Grandfather firmly. "When they comes all tangled in the nets, don't just chop off their noses and throw 'em back—bring 'em in, see? Gut 'em and split 'em, hang 'em to dry. Bake 'em in the oven when ya wants to use 'em. Warm 'em till the oil comes out, then give 'em to the dogs. That's why we calls 'em dogfish, see, 'cause we used to feed 'em to . . . the dogs."

Grandfather's eyelids drooped.

The men looked at each other.

"Calamari," said one fisherman, getting back to the squid.

"Kraken," said another.

"I minds there was a big squid sunk a schooner once," said Daniel Squires quickly.

"Oh, you'll not be tellin' that old yarn ag'in'," said Theophilous irritably, taking a plug of chewing tobacco out of his jacket pocket.

"'Tis no yarn at all, Theophilous Piccot, just cold and sober facts," said Daniel. "And you'll need to be cuttin' me half a letter of that chaw to make up fer yer mistrustful atty-tude."

Theophilous grumbled but cut anyway, nipping through the black stick of compressed tobacco leaf. BEAVER CHAW, the full brand name read, and Daniel Squires got most of the piece under the letter "R."

"'Twas the schooner *Pearl*," he said, "pretty a packet as ever sailed the Indian Ocean." He raised his hands and paused a moment. Tom imagined the tall-masted, white-sailed ship and the cries of her doomed men.

"The captain, he spies something loomin' up on the water, and he tries to figure what it is. A big, low bank of weed, maybe? But that don't seem right. He asks the first mate what he thinks, and the first mate answers, ' 'Ceptin' for her size, and color, and the way she is built—might be a whale,' 'cause he'd never seed nothin' like it neither.

"'Get me my rifle,' says the captain to the cabin boy.

"Then Bill Darling, second mate, sings out from the riggin', 'I wouldn't be doin' that, Captain,' says he. 'That there is a squid and will sink us,' he says. And Bill Darling, he was a Newfoundland man."

"Aarrh." Everyone nodded at this. A Newfoundland man. He'd know what to do.

"But the captain, he's proud and foolish; he just laughs.

"Bill Darling climbs down from where he was up in the shrouds, where he's been tyin' a sail, and the cabin boy comes up wi' the weapon. The captain, he's kept 'er all loaded heavy—five fingers of powder and three of heavy shot—and he squints and takes aim at that monstrous squid.

"*Bang!* He lets fly. A big hole opens up in the flesh on the back of the beast. The kraken, he turns and rushes at them, movin' jerky like squids do, but fast, faster than anythin'. They has them things underneath, ye knows, as lets squid suck in water and spit it out fast.

"'Get axes and swords. It's goin' to board us,' yells Bill Darling (and him a good Newfoundland man). The men rush around, but all they can find is one ax and two swords, and Bill Darling, he grabs a sword.

"The squid comes at 'em tail on, but then it flips over, end for end, and them two longest harns—I guess they'm arms, really—they stretches up the side o' the *Pearl.*

"One arm grabs poor Bill and squashes him 'gainst the mainmast. And t'other long arm reaches high in the shrouds, takin' a hold o' the riggin'.

"And the last words they heard from Bill Darling was 'Slash fer yer lives, b'ys; he's comin' aboard!'"

Daniel Squires paused and spat expertly; the stream of tobacco juice arched neatly to the white chamber pot beside the bed.

Tom thought about the giant squid pulling its weight up the side of the ship. In his mind he saw the schooner start to lean. Leaning, leaning . . .

"Then the cargo shifts belowdeck," said Daniel Squires. "Boxes and ballast, all slides to one side."

"She'll tip!" said Tom. "She'll turn over, sure!"

"And tip she did," said Daniel Squires, nodding. "The *Pearl* went over on her side, so's water got into the cargo hold. She filled up, and the squid—he pulled that schooner down."

"You 'lows that can't be true," said Theophilous.

"The *Pearl* went down," insisted Daniel. "And the survivors was picked up by a warship what seen the whole thing, too. The captain lived, and the story was writ up in the *London Times* paper herself." He nodded, the story thus being officially confirmed. Though almost none of the men could read (or perhaps because of this), anything in print was regarded as unquestionable truth.

"But what happened to Bill Darling?" Tom wanted to hear, as if he had never heard the tale before.

"He was never seen nor heard from again. The monster took him down," said Daniel.

"Kraken," said Grandfather. "Kraken. Biggest fish that grows in the sea. They eats whales, I hear, or maybe 'tis t'other way round, I don't know.

"But I minds when I was a youngster, out on the Grand Banks we found one o' them gert big squids. The kraken. It was dead, floatin' when we found 'im. Had a beak could nip off yer head. One o' the arms was so big took two men to carry it. We chopped up the carcass and brought 'im home. Used 'im to manure the potato fields."

His eyes shut. Having had the last word on the subject, as usual, Grandfather went to sleep. The room emptied then, and most of the people went home. Some of the ladies stayed on to help if there was need.

"Time fer you to be nappin', Tom," said Ma.

He protested bedtime, as was his habit. Ma paid no attention, as was hers. Baby Sally and Mark Josephus were already gone, he realized. Lynny, too.

When he had shucked off his outer clothing and in longjohns climbed into his bed, he tried to tell his mother about the dog.

"I can't be feedin' no dogs," she said, whispering so as not to wake Mark Josephus in the other bed.

"Murphy could pull wood fer Skipper, and Grandfather says we could feed him on useless old dogfish," said Tom. "And Ma, Ma, he stuck up fer me! Murphy was all barkin' at the monster! He wasn't feared or nothin'!"

"I've got no food to feed him, son," she said, "even now, let alone when we hit the starvin' time. Say yer prayers."

Tom's prayers that night were even shorter than usual.

"Dear God," he said, sitting up in bed, "please help Grandfather be all right. And also let Ma change her mind about me new dog, on account o' Ma bein' so nice. Murphy would be such a help to the family, and pull wood, and take care o' Baby Sally and Mark Josephus and Lynny, and would hardly eat at all. The dog, I mean, not Lynny. You know what she eats like. Oh, and best wishes to Your Boy, Lord Skipper, Him what made the storm get quiet for the fishermen that time, and bless Peter and Paul and them others, 'specially Bill Darling, him as got took by the squid. Good night, Lord, and I hopes You has a good sleep. Amen."

Ma snorted, tucked Tom in tight, and kissed him on the forehead.

The door shut behind her. The scuff of slippers faded down the canvas-covered hall. Tom loosened the blankets that Ma always snugged up as if to choke him.

Then Tom remembered a request he'd forgotten to put in his prayer.

He listened to his brother's breathing, making sure Mark Josephus was asleep and wouldn't hear.

"I wants to add somethin', Lord Skipper," he said, quiet as he could. His hands even folded to underline this next request's importance:

"If it ain't too much trouble, don't be sendin' me no more o' them big squids, nor krakens, whatever they'm called."

He paused, then added, "Aside from little ones that I can use fer bait."

Outside, the winds of Newfoundland shrieked and howled and gusted and whispered.

The rain stopped.

Tom was asleep.

CHAPTER THREE

"ARE YE FREEMAN, OR A SLAVE?"

◆   ◆   ◆

Rock cracked. Green flames shot up, and through them clutching tentacles reached—for Grandfather! Tom tried to shout a warning, but no words came. The kraken's arms wrapped around the old man, who surprisingly did not seem worried. He only smiled and said, "Keep t' family goin'." The monster dragged him down, and the old man gestured with his pipe and said, "I'm dependin' on ya."

Tom sat up quickly, blue eyes gone wide, looking to see if Old Hag Nightmare were crouched on his chest about to steal his breath, as legend told.

Pale sunlight flooded the room. Why had nobody wakened him, nobody told him to go make the fire? Not that he minded the chance to sleep. The chill of cold air made him wiggle back under the down comforter. He listened.

Even the winds were still. Only the peaceful sound of Mark Josephus's breathing in the other bed disturbed the quiet. It was past time to get up, but if nobody minded, why should he complain?

Nightmare faded, Tom closed his eyes, snuggling into the warmth and coziness, the sleepiness of half-awake, then—

The next thought woke him completely.

"Grandfather!"

He was out of bed and across the room, bare feet racing down the canvas-covered hallway, through the kitchen, up the staircase.

He burst into Grandfather's room. "Wake up, Grandfather! Sun's high, and—"

A white cloth lay over the face and body of a man on the bed. The cloth was beautiful. It had a broad black cross on the middle and intricately scalloped lace along the edge. It was used only once in any man's life.

"No!" Tom snatched the burial linen back.

It was Grandfather, yet it was not. The eyes half-open, the mouth gone slack.

Gentle hands were on Tom's shoulders, and half-heard voices soothed. The burial cloth was taken gently from his fingers and replaced.

"No, no!" Tom shouted. "He can't be! He's just asleep! He has to hear the eider ducks. He was tellin' me how they always brings the first big snow. We're goin' troutin' afore school starts!"

"He's in a better place now, Tom," said Ma.

"What? Heaven? Harps and that? He don't play music! He don't want no heaven. He wants to be here, wi' me, to go troutin'!"

Daniel Squires's gentle voice broke in. "There's troutin'

in the good place, too, b'y, sure there is, and you'll fish wi' him again, bye and bye—jest can't be wi' him for a while, that's all—and hey, he's got all his teeth now, don't need to mash up his bacon wi' his fark no more."

"We just has to accept it, son," said Ma. "Got to be like the grass that bends wi' the wind, not a tree that's too stiff and gets broke."

Lynny grabbed and squeezed her brother's fingers hard, as if to hurt away the greater pain.

Theophilous Piccot said nothing at all. He only sat and stared, red-eyed, taking no part in the fuss around him, as if he and his dad were alone in the room.

"Grampa?" came the high, sweet voice. "What are ya doin' there, under the covers? Is ya hidin' from me?" asked Baby Sally, coming into the room.

There is little dirt in Newfoundland. Glaciers took it long ago. The rivers of ice, having scraped the soil off the land, dumped it into the sea.

This mass movement of earth made the ocean rich, farming difficult, and burials interesting.

BUHHHWHOOOM! The packed gunpowder blew, expanding a crack in the bedrock granite. Chips flew in all directions, high on the hill and into the waters of the cove. One head-sized chunk flew a hundred feet up, to tumble and fall down, at last, right in the Piccots' front yard.

"Grave's dug," said Daniel Squires as Tom unplugged his ears, then scrambled up from the ground where he lay.

The gunpowder smell brought back memories. He and Grandfather had once been on an island trip to hunt seabirds packed in thousands on their breeding ground. Grandfather had stood purposefully in front of a soft snowbank. He had the big rifle so jampacked with powder that he knew it would knock him over backward. It did, and when he got up after the blast, twelve of the gray, red-eyed turrs lay still and senseless before them—all except one, which flapped in pain till Grandfather knocked it down and stepped quick on its head.

"Let nothin' suffer," he said. "Kill what ya need and waste naught."

And today, as they picked out the rocks from the grave, Tom remembered a time when Grandfather would *not* shoot.

They had come on a herd of caribou: brown, velvet-antlered, knee-clicking, smelly reindeer, a hundred or more. Tom wanted him to blast away, but Grandfather said, "Can't do 'er. I'm loaded with shot; I might cripple five or six, and they'd go off and die, slow and sufferin', no good to anyone."

Everywhere Tom went that day, it seemed he bumped into memories of Grandfather.

When it came time to wash for the funeral and he crouched shivering in the washtub, soaping and sponging quick as he could in the misery of a midweek bath, he was almost angry about it. Bad enough to go through this once a week on Saturday night, need it or not.

But then as he toweled dry behind the screen, he spotted his well-worn yellow oilskins hanging on their hook by the door. And he remembered his first set of oilskins. He had been six years old.

Ma had sewn the pants and shirt from flour sacks and calico, but the work after that was for Tom. As Grandfather put it, in a voice that allowed no argument, "A fisherman worth keepin' does his own oilskins."

So Tom had burnt the linseed oil, cooking it on the Waterloo stove till the liquid was thick and yellow in the pan. Then, carefully, he took the hot pan out back into the attached storage shed. He poured the gluey stuff onto the jacket and pants, soaking the cloth much as it would hold. Then he laid a piece of brown paper on the floor, set the oil-soaked clothes on top of that, and put more paper over them. Grandfather helped him rock a big flour barrel over the top of the homemade sea clothes. The weight of the barrel would press the oil into the cloth so it became waterproof. In a week the process had to be repeated—oil, soaking, pressing—and again the following week, and again, and again. But when a month was over, Tom had his own yellow oilskins like a regular Newfoundland fisherman.

Tom sighed and reached for his clothes.

When it was time, the family walked to the church and sat in their regular place. Tom saw the coffin his father had made with the death cloth on it now.

Silence deepened. After a while Tom got bored. He rocked on his seat and remembered the one and only time Grandfather ever hit him.

It began with a bunch of raisins, which are called figs in Newfoundland. Tom purely loved the sugar-sweet dried fruit, considering them a present from heaven, a personal gift from the Skipper in the sky.

Oh, sweet lassy buns, or boiled raisin pudding (called figgy duff), or just the plain figs by themselves! He even liked how they stuck between his teeth so they lasted a good long time.

Raisins were also, well, portable. They almost jumped into his pocket. Nobody seemed to notice. Tom knew food was often short, and you were supposed to ask before taking a snack. But he figured Ma was busy, and there was no sense bothering her about something so unimportant. His new raisin system worked very well until one morning . . .

Ten-year-old Tom was just pulling up his trousers when a bunch of yesterday's raisins, somehow uneaten, tipped out of his pocket onto the floor.

"I thought I was runnin' low on the figs," said Ma, frowning. "I ain't been makin' that many duffs."

"This has happened before?" asked Grandfather.

Ma looked at Tom, who was still wondering how he could have overlooked the raisins.

Grandfather sighed. "Get yer jacket, b'y," he said.

They stepped outside into the quiet, settled snow of midwinter. A few hundred yards down the hill and up the path was a stand of alders not thick enough for serious wooding.

When they got there, Grandfather handed Tom his knife. "Cut me a switch about three feet long, thick as my thumb."

Tom did as he was told, knowing now what he was here for. His friends were all raised with the switch or the strap, and he had sometimes wondered how he was lucky enough to be spared. He handed over the heavy stick. Grandfather took the knife and pared away the bark and stubs. He whistled it once through the air. It made an ugly whooshing sound. Tom was flat terrified.

"Bend over. Keep yer hands outta the way," Grandfather said.

Tom gritted his teeth and studied the snow beneath his boots.

There was the whooshing noise again, then *thwop!* For a second Tom felt nothing at all, as if the sting had been stopped by his clothes. Then the impact struck like a line of red fire. The pain shot deep and wrapped around, seeming to cut through muscle and bone. Tom quickly straightened up, grabbed where it hurt, and jumped up and down to relieve his emotion.

Grandfather set the stick down, but Tom noticed it was within reach. Grandfather lit his pipe. "That's how I was raised, b'y," he said, "and it ain't a good way. Hurts a man inside to get beat on. I won't even beat no dog, let alone a human person. If I was to have a dog ag'in, which I can't 'count o' yer ma bein' so set agin' 'em, I wouldn't never raise no stick to 'im. I would just do like this—" he reached his hand, thumb and circled forefinger cupping under Tom's chin, and lifted his hand so Tom's teeth clicked together, not hard but surprising— "and then I'd say *NO!* real sharp. Don't really hurt, but it don't feel good. Do that when yer animal does somethin' wrong. He'll learn what *NO!* means, and after that just the word is enough if ya give 'em good habits."

"Why do Ma hate dogs so much?" Tom wanted to know.

"Well, 'cause one time she—don't be changin' the subject!

"Anyways, see, in the old country people used to be like slaves. A few people owned ever'thin', and the rest of us, we owned nothin' at all. Even the roof over our head, that belonged to somebody else, he that owned the land. Hard to explain . . ." He puffed his pipe for a moment.

"Now s'posin', b'y, that you was hungry, and there was no food in the house. What would ya do?"

"Catch me a fish, o' course," Tom said shortly. What a stupid question!

"No such of a thing. Back then, if ya took the leetlest fish or a rabbit or anythin' at all, that was stealin', poachin', see, and you could have yer hands cut off fer it. Growed men or childern either could be whipped or hung or branded. I minds me a man had a *S T* scar branded on one cheek—*S T* stood fer Sheep Thief.

"That was how it used to be in the old country. But then I heard about Newfoundland, *our* Newfoundland, from a fishin' servant that was goin' over there. He said as how here things was different, and a man could own his place and live comfortable all his days, s'posin' he worked. So I come over. Didn't have nothin', just me clothes, and I had to work five years in a St. John's fish house once I got here, just to pay fer the voyage across.

"But one day I'll never fergit. The man comes to me and says, 'You can go about yer business now.' Simple as that. The debt was paid off. I could go anywhere I wanted to.

"I walked over here t' Portugal Cove 'cause I knowed about this place by now, and I got me some handline and hooks from the merchant on credit. Traded 'im some Christmas fish I got fer nothin' under the ice. It wasn' easy some days. I slept under a dory fer a spell, but I worked shares fer a fisherman, and then I bought me own nets.

"Winters I worked cuttin' timber, and I saved some wood, see, cuttin' on the halves—half fer me, half fer the St. John's merchant—till I had enough fer me house. One year I got the debt so low, the merchant, he give me credit to get that Waterloo stove. Fine thing a stove is, better'n a fireplace, keeps the weather outta your bones.

"I married yer Grandma. You niver knowed 'er. She—" He looked out across the hills, across the years.

"Well, times was good fer a long while. We had actual money, cash money you could touch in yer hand, none o' them credit slips. We saved some o' it, too. How we saved! In a St. John's thing they calls a bank.

"Yessir, fer a while we was almost rich. Before I took and put some o' that money in a ship, we had us eighteen hunnert pounds."

Tom whistled. Such a sum was beyond his imagining. "In money? What happened to it? How come we ain't rich now? Where is the ship?"

The old man was quiet. Then he shook his head. "Gone—money, the ship—all gone. Things happens sometimes that ya don't plan on. They just . . . happens.

"Well, the point is, here in this country we got a chance. It ain't perfect—nothin' is—but we got a chance. Get hungry? Go catch a fish or a rabbit, and nobody'll raise a hand to ya. 'Tis deeficult, o' course. If 'twas easy, all could do 'er. But long as we sticks by our own and looks out fer each other, well, we has a chance, and that's all a man can hope fer."

Grandfather's gaze came back to Tom, who shivered suddenly. The blue eyes searched him, and Grandfather was not smiling. He picked up the stick and touched Tom on the shoulder. "What I needs to know is, are ya a free man that can be trusted and will stand beside his own, keep the family safe—not *steal* from them." Tom looked at the snow. "Or are ya a slave that can only learn from the stick?"

"I'd be a free man and care fer me folks," said Tom, and he raised his eyes and left off rubbing.

"Yis, b'y," said Grandfather, "I knowed ya would be like that, once ya thought on it a while." And he broke the stick and tossed it.

The welt disappeared in a week. But the memory, like the encounter with the kraken, would linger in his mind always.

Tom shifted on the church bench and tried to stay awake to show respect for the man who was gone. The words the preacher spoke were important, no doubt, but after thirty minutes or so Tom could hear the rustle of clothing, the rumble of Lynny's stomach, anything that broke the endless, numbing torrent of big words. He smelled the cedar of the coffin boards and wished he had some spruce gum to chew. He loved how the yellow balls of hardened sap first turned powdery in his mouth, then went stringy, and finally settled into a chewy, long-lasting, refreshing wad.

He looked at Rosie down the aisle. That sure was some pretty bonnet. Funny how he had never noticed before how her hair poked out from underneath it so nice. Then Rosie looked his way and saw Tom seeing her. Both snapped instantly back to the preacher, deeply interested in whatever it was he'd been talking about.

Beside Tom, Mark Josephus sat bolt upright, genuinely involved in the sermon. He loved this kind of stuff. Baby Sally was being exceptionally good, too, needing only to be found and retrieved four times so far.

Then Sarah Chadbourne's long nose twitched. The nostrils flared. She made quick little sniffs, not for breath, but to detect scent information.

Ma nudged Theo, who glanced quickly at Sarah.

Daniel Squires leaned forward. "Sarah's nose is twitchin'," he said.

Theo sighed.

The preacher picked up on the crowd's sudden inattention and began to hurry, but he still had a lot to say and remembered still more, until at last Sarah Chadbourne stood up. It might be church, it might be a burying, but she had her duty to do.

"Pardon, Your Reverence. Ladies, we be goin' to have a bit of a dwigh," she said.

"I'm sorry fer yer trouble," she said to Marian and Theo. They nodded, understanding fully.

With that the congregation rose. Everyone was heading for the back door.

"Fine sermon, Reverend."

"Wonnerful, wish we could stay and hear the rest."

"Sorry fer yer troubles, Missuz Piccot, ma'am."

"We'll be back and help wi' the lowerin' later, but ya see how it is."

"Sorry fer yer troubles, Marian, Theo. He was a good man, a fine fish-killer."

Then the church was empty, all except old George in his usual place in the middle, second row from the front. As George put it, "I be in the fall of the leaf and no good fer the ocean no more." At 103, it was understood that George was excused from most work, not being as spry as his son who was, after all, only 82. Besides, George purely loved sermons. Wherefore he leaned forward now and rapped his old knuckles on the empty pew before him, prompting the minister. "You was sayin', Your Excellency?"

"Oh yes. Umm, we here must always remember—"

Outside, Tom broke into a run. He snatched a quick look at the sky but did not slow. Everyone else was doing the same: ladies in long dresses; men in suits with stiff, white collars; boys and girls dressed the same, but smaller; and every mother's child of them running in their Sunday best—to fight for their lives.

CHAPTER FOUR

"And Those Who Starve . . ."

◆   ◆   ◆

Tom was listening for one small and terrible sound, a tiny noise almost meaningless to outsiders. If Sarah Chadbourne's nose was right, a dwigh was on the way, deadly to the village as acid poured from the sky. Maybe, just this once, Sarah's nose would be wrong?

Plipppp.

Tom heard the sound of the water droplet hitting. Just a raindrop, all it was.

But it landed on a two-by-three-foot open chunk of fish, an amber-gold slab of drying codfish steak. Hand-salted cod, famous around the world because it could last six months in a barrel and still bake up nutritious and fine. This quality came of back-breaking hours of catching, clean- ing, wash-and-salting, and turning the cod over and over to catch just the right amount of sun. Now that fish lay flat and open, defenseless against the rain.

The dwigh was just a brief rain shower.

But any fish the rain hit would be down-graded, perhaps ruined for sale. The fine-grained flesh would spot, beginning the process of rot—the village's hope of survival turning into slime.

Villagers raced to the "flakes," flattened spruce boughs on which the drying fish lay. Every child old enough not to fall off the stage and every oldster still able to bend over helped.

Tom snatched up flat, thick triangles of fish until his arms could hold no more. He stacked this armful, or "yaffle," in a pile, top fish in each pile placed skin up—for whatever protection that could offer—then yaffled up another and another.

Baby Sally staggered with one fish almost as long as she was. Mark Josephus carried two.

"Every pound's a help!" yelled Daniel Squires, encouraging the children.

"Tom, get the rinds!" shouted Theo, but Tom was already snatching up the flattened sections of bark, home-made shields to fight the rain.

Every fish must be stacked, and every stack covered; that's what the rinds were for.

Bend and grab, yaffle the fish, lift and twist and set them in a stack, grab a rind and cover them, then go get some more. Hurry!

It was desperate work, done at absolute top speed in the steadily increasing rain.

And yet there was an element of joy in it, for the people were united, working together. Quick as any family finished stacking and covering their own fish, they turned to help their neighbors. They worked as one, a people with their minds made up. Stronger than this, there is nothing on earth.

When at last the full force of the rain came down, sluicing in battering torrents, it fell upon a hundred little white bark roofs, like tiny houses.

Everyone was sopping wet, but they laughed, triumphant in the rain. Their fish were safe.

The few cod that had gotten spotted with water damage would be re-salted with brine and put aside for personal use, to be eaten soon.

Theo, Daniel, and five or six others absented themselves to lower the coffin. That had to be done before the rain filled up the grave. They would have to pile up rocks afterward, too, to keep the coffin from washing away. It would be awkward to say good-bye to a loved one and then meet him later, drifting in from the bay.

Tom looked for Rosie. There she was with her mother, the Widow Crandall, whose husband had been dead three years, ever since he'd gone to Labrador on a sealing ship and been crushed in the ice.

"Shall we go back to church now?" asked Rosie of her ma.

"Oh, aye, we sure do look some pretty," laughed her mother, whose black dress was soaked from the rain.

Then faintly there came a sound that promised fun: two semi-musical notes, the first low, the next high.

Too-ooo! The noise came from an exceedingly dented brass horn, blown by a man who knew much about horses and nothing of music.

Too-ooo! The coach!

"Can I go, Skipper?" Tom asked his father.

"Aye, get t' cent!" said Lynny.

"Don't rip yer clothes!" said his mother, with the look of one who knows her words are wasted.

"Candy!" put in Baby Sally, who had shared in Tom's winnings before.

"Yes, yes!"

"Me, too!" agreed Mark Josephus, who considered eating one of life's most sacred joys. "A peppermint knob and a bull's-eye and—"

Tom was already gone.

Every so often a coach with two horses drove over the hills all the way from St. John's, twelve kilometers to Portugal Cove. As nobody but the rich could afford such luxury (and they usually had luggage to carry), the coach's arrival meant the possibility of a coin flung to the strongest, luckiest kid. The boys went into a frenzy of competition for the broad red Newfoundland cent, or even the ha'penny (half cent)—actual cash money! True, you had to go to St. John's to spend it, but a half cent bought a belly-filling lot.

There was only one path the stage could take, and Tom knew where it would come over the hill.

It was all uphill from the wharf to the lodge, where rich visitors always stayed. His lungs burned, but his legs were swift. He matched his energies against the wind and the rain and the other running boys. He was just ahead of Jimmy Anderson when the coach came over the top of the rise.

Tom made his feet trade places faster and faster, risking a slip on the thin coat of mud over rock.

The coach was almost beside them—going too fast. Jimmy Anderson slowed, pulled up, knew he'd missed it. Tom kept running.

There was a big erratic by the coach's path, and this

huge boulder left by the glaciers had sort of a step on it, where children sometimes climbed. With hardly time to think, Tom ran up on the eight-foot rock and leaped, diving full out, hands high and clutching.

His body slammed against the back of the coach, which rocked on its springs and wood wheels. He slid—for a moment thinking he would fall—then his fingers grasped the luggage rack, and he was safe.

His feet found the low footman's standbar, and Tom relaxed and yelled for sheer delight.

The small curtained window with scarlet waterproof curtains was just in front of Tom. A hand appeared there. The hand wore three jeweled rings, and the wrist above it showed a white silk sleeve and a purple brocade jacket. The curtain slid back. Tom looked into the face of—a boy? Older than Tom but not entirely a man yet, he had cold gray eyes, a pointed nose, and thin lips that twisted in a general distaste for the inferior world.

Their eyes locked.

Then the coach hit a pothole. Tom should have expected it, having ridden on the back of the coach twice before, but he was distracted and lost his grip.

Up and off to the side he flew, landing on his side on the rock and the mud. He rolled over twice and came up on one knee. He'd been soaked before, now he was filthy. And of course the knee of his pants was ripped. Ma's not gonna be too happy about that, he thought, getting up.

But the coach stopped before it reached the lodge.

A short, plaindressed woman clambered down, not waiting for help, which was just as well, none being offered. She had a large brown paper package with her, wrapped in string, the way outporters carried their luggage on the rare occasions they traveled.

She's one of we, thought Tom, amazed to see a regular person who had ridden on the coach.

The woman shut the door, and the driver went on, barely giving her time to get out of the way.

She ran to Tom, who was shaky but on his feet. His hands were scraped, and there was blood mixed with the mud.

"Is you all right, boy?" she said. Then "Tom!"

Tom looked, and looked again. "Peggeen?" She was his older sister's best friend. Round, red-faced, cheery Peggeen Wilder looked strong and was.

"Aye, 'tis me! Is ya hurt much? What a brave leap it was!"

"I'm fine," said Tom, "'cept me clothes. But where did ya spring from? Last I heard you was livin' in St. John's, goin' to school or some such."

"I did, and I'm done. I'm the new schoolteacher," she said happily.

"Yer a teacher? Naw. Ya don't mean it. Woman can't be no teacher!" said Tom, astonished.

"Why not?" said Peggeen.

"Well, because . . . because women always stays home and does chores around the house. That's how it is."

"Just because something is doesn't mean it is right, and the only way," said Peggeen.

"There's things I do better than cookin' and cleanin' and sewin' and stuff. Not to mention I hates all that junk. But teachin' I loves."

Tom shook his head. This would take getting used to. "But if you'm the new schoolteacher, what about old fatty, Whipper Treadwell?" he asked.

"'E had a heart attack an' died!"

"Hah!" Tom laughed and clapped his hands, too honest to pretend sadness at the death of a very mean man.

"Now, be nice!" said Peggeen, but she smiled just the same. She knew what Whipper Treadwell had been.

The coach was stopping outside the lodge a couple hundred yards away. And for this passenger, the driver got down and bowed as he touched the handle of the door.

From the house there came a scurry of motion. The owner himself came running out with a shawl outstretched before him. Behind him came the maids, cook's helpers, and the cook, all standing stiff and straight in the rain, waiting to greet this important visitor.

The coach door opened. An elegant buckled shoe emerged slowly. The leg below the golden pants was clad in pure white stocking.

The boy who stepped out was as large as a man. He looked fat at first, but did not move that way. He was just big, balancing himself athletically, and his shoulders were heavy under the gorgeous coat.

The owner bowed and offered the shawl to protect the rich boy from the rain.

But the stranger unfolded something handled and dark beside him, something Tom had never seen before. It was a portable shelter from the rain, beginning narrow, becoming wide, and this (whatever it was) the boy opened and handed to the merchant, who obligingly if awkwardly held it over his visitor's head as they walked together to the house. The newcomer did not trouble himself to notice the servants standing in the wet.

"What's that?"

"'E calls it an umberelly," said Peggeen. "Handy thing, ain't it? Be good to keep the fish dry, were it big enough."

"No, I meant the other, the fat boy."

"Whipper Treadwell's nephew, the merchant's son," Peggeen answered. "Edmund is his name, I think. 'E's been over at England takin' school. 'Ain't 'e grand?"

"What's 'e like?"

Peggeen shook her head. "Ain't right to judge too quick, but 'e 'minds me of rotten sugar cake," she said, "pretty to look at, but poison inside."

Boy, owner, and servants disappeared inside the lodge.

"Come to the house fer supper, Lynny'll be crazy glad to see ya," said Tom, and a daughter of the outport village was home.

Two days later Tom and Theo were working in their front yard. Theo sawed wood, and Tom was chopping splits.

Murphy was walking around the fenced yard, and Tom was wishing he would go back under the house. The dog was still a sore subject. Tom had been feeding him cod heads and fish guts, whatever could be found, and Marian Piccot was not speaking to her son. Surprisingly, Theo had argued in favor of the dog.

"Got some plans fer the winter," he'd said. "We'll give the dog a try. But 'e's yours, Tom, and nobody else's," he warned. "If you don't feed 'im, 'e starves. And if 'e kills a goat or steals any of our food, well, you minds the story of the four dogs and the needle."

"Yis, Skipper," Tom had said. He knew the story. How in a village up the coast, one of a family's four dogs had swallowed a good sewing needle. Nobody knew which dog had swallowed it, just that the needle was gone, dropped in the yard while the dogs were about. This happened in summer, when dogs were not much needed, their chief value being the pulling of sleds. The needle, however, was irreplaceable. They couldn't get another until the merchant's ship returned. So the four dogs, one by one, were killed. The needle was found in the fourth dog's stomach.

Murphy stopped and looked out to sea. Tom followed his gaze.

And there it was. At the mouth of Portugal Cove.

"The clipper!"

High sails of white canvas, sweet lines of dark wood, beautiful and strong—the merchant's ship.

Aboard would be all manner of wonderful stuff: hogshead barrels full of salted pork; puncheons of molasses and rum; flour and sugar; tobacco and cloth; as well as incredible luxuries, like apples and candy, oranges and shoelaces. All you needed to get into that wonderland of practically anything you could think of was the merchant-approved credit slip marked with however much value he said your fish was worth . . .

"Clipper's to port!"

"I heared ya t' first time," said Theophilous, pausing with the saw. "But it's no nevermind, not fer couple three hours or so. 'Twill take 'em at least that long to set up. Time enough then to see how they'll cheat us."

It was settling-up time. Today the village's future was decided: a year's work measured, the winter's food offered—or refused.

Tom caught the length of sawed wood his dad tossed him, then set it on the tree stump. Swooping down the "tom-hawk," he split the chunk in half.

"'Nother junk," warned Theo before tossing the next.

Tom caught it midair, set it on the chopping block, and sank the hand ax all in one motion, quick as he could without chopping his hand. This one had a knot in the middle and would not split all the way. He turned it upside down, hatchet still in, and thumped them both down. This time the wood split cleanly, separating around the knot.

Winter was almost on them. They would need to have

lots of wood for warmth, cooking, and the heating of water—the fires always ate the wood too fast.

Soon not much work would be going on in the cove. "Fish in summer, play in winter" was the old saying. If the fishing went well and the merchants traded them enough food, winter might be bad as it wished, with the people snug and warm inside. They would settle down, take things easy, give exhausted bodies a rest.

But if a family "had no summer" and caught not enough fish to trade for supplies, their only hope was to trap rabbits or catch Christmas fish through the ice, and depend on help from their neighbors.

Nobody had very much to help with. To the people of the outports "poor" did not mean empty wallets or the absence of luxury. That was how they lived. "Poor" meant you were dead.

Everything depended on today.

The ship at harbor hoisted the commerce flag. They were ready to inspect the year's catch.

"'Tis time," said Theophilous, and he put the saw under a birch rind to keep the tool safe from rain. Tom saw his father's face was set, the muscles in his jaws clenched tight. He looked pale, almost ill.

This was the first settling-up at which Grandfather would not be there to argue for them. It was all on Theo's shoulders now. Well, Tom thought, I'll stand beside him like he stood by Grandfather.

They carried the cured fish down from the twine loft, using the flat carry boards called hand sledges. A quintal of dried fish, 112 pounds, was a load. It took ninety-nine trips before they got it all down, plus what was already there on the docks. Ma and Theo worked together, as did Tom and Daniel Squires. Even so it took fully two hours to lug the fish down.

Tom could not help noticing how fine their fish were. Nobody made fish as good as the Piccots. At every step in the preparation of the cod, they had taken the extra trouble and effort that added up to a quality fish. For one thing alone, there was hardly a flyspeck on the whole lot. Credit for that went to Baby Sally and Mark Josephus, who had waved spruce limbs to keep the hard-biting black flies away. They had a clean and beautiful season's worth of fish, prime and wholesome, subtly delicious.

The judging of the fish would be done inside the community store on a large open floor reserved for the purpose.

The Anderson family had lived longest in the cove, so they would go first. The Piccots were next, so they stood at the door. Tom idly scratched Murphy's head. "I should have left ya home," he said. "Whatever ya do, don't mess wi' the fish." The big Newfoundland wagged his tail and looked straight up at Tom as if he understood.

Outside all was motion. The folks brought their fish to this point, and the merchant's sailors would take it from there, bringing it in for the merchant's inspection and from there out to the ship. Some of the sailors were outport men, too, and the people were talking to them.

They had had more fish last year, Tom knew, watching the sailors bring in the Piccot piles—not that last year had been wonderful, nor the year before. There just were not many fish to catch. Nobody had done really well, and this year Grandfather had been too sick to help much.

James Anderson the elder came out glumly, holding a white slip of paper in one hand. He looked at it and shook his head. "It's yeer turn now," he said to the Piccots, "and may ye have better luck than me."

Skinny James Anderson the younger waved at Tom, and Mrs. Anderson stopped to say hello to Ma.

"Stay, Murphy," said Tom. Murphy settled down outside and closed his eyes.

Inside was quiet. There were tables at one end behind which the merchants and their help sat on extra-fancy chairs, high ones, decked out to look like palace thrones. There were three people sitting on the chairs today: the fat rich boy Tom had seen on the coach; a clerk with the account book, heavy with the ink of men's lives; and Archibald Simons, junior partner of the firm of Treadwell and Treadwell.

Nobody liked Merchant Simons, a tight-fisted little man, narrow and cold, but at least he was a familiar threat. Folks knew what he was about and had learned to live with him. The clerk, of course, just did as he was told. But the large-built boy? Nobody knew what he was about. He was an unknown element except for his name. His father owned the company. Edmund Treadwell had power.

There was also a fourth man, important, although he did not rate a chair. He was the culler, an ex-fisherman, paid to judge and "cull" the fish, separating them by quality. Normally he worked behind a special raised table, examining each fish one by one, poking and prodding, testing with his thumb, checking such things as whether the cod meat was breakable (which meant too much salt) or reddish in color (which meant not enough). Often the culler would talk constantly, making happy chit-chat so that the fisherman would not argue over the grading of every fish.

Normally there were five grades of fish—like schooling grades A to F—from best to worst. Excellent was merchantable (large and small), then came Madeira, West Indies, and tomcod (or cullage), which last was unacceptable, good only for personal use. It was right that the cod should be graded. Some people worked harder to make better fish, and quality should be rewarded.

But today there was no arguing. The culler was silent and never looked up. He squatted briefly beside every pile, breaking it down with quick flicks of the wrist, fast as he could move. Each pile became two, one considerably larger than the other. Two sailors followed after him, restacking the yaffles into carryable neatness.

Oh, no, Tom thought, only two piles, and the one pile really small? They're judging *tal qual*: just two grades of fish, good and bad. No credit would be given for the best fish, the kind the Piccots made.

"And where is your father?" asked the merchant as they waited for the culler to finish.

"We buried him three days ago."

"Sorry for your trouble," said Archibald Simons, but his eyes did not lift from the fish.

"Ahh, but where are my manners?" he said, indicating the white-wigged boy beside him, all sprawled on his chair as if he were half-asleep. His chair was the plushest of the three, and he did not trouble to sit up.

"This is Master Edmund, son of our beloved owner," said merchant Archibald Simons. "Master Edmund is just back from school in England. He has learned the most up-to-date marketing skills and is here to share them with us. He will be a most valuable asset to the Treadwell and Treadwell codfish establishment. Master Edmund, Theophilous Piccot."

"I looks to you and I smiles," said Theophilous politely, and he extended his hand.

Edmund did not appear to notice. He did, however, nod his white-wigged head. The powdered wig made him look older, which was the intended effect. Edmund wore velvet breeches today, a delicate handwoven silk shirt, and calf-high boots of hand-tooled leather. A cloak hung carelessly over the back of his chair, like a robe tossed onto a throne.

"And this is me boy, Tom," said Theo.

Edmund did not quite yawn.

Tom said nothing.

The merchant rubbed his thin hands together. They made a dry hissing noise.

"Well, down to business! Bad news, I fear, Theophilous. But I'm sure you know that already, with both the quality and quantity of your catch so low this year."

"What do ya mean, low quality?" said Theophilous, looking stunned. "I grant ya, it ain't three hundred quintal, such as we could catch years ago—ain't been many fish—but that there is prime. Not a sunburned fish in the lot, and ye see how nice the saltin' was done. Sure, 'tis all merchantable, not a fish there less than prime Madeira grade."

"I grant you it isn't *all* cullage," said the merchant, making a face, "but most of it is only suited for the West Indies trade—those people don't know good fish anyway. But I'll tell you what I'll do. I've been friends with your father these many years, and for old times' sake—oh, I'm cheating myself, I know—I'll give thirty-three pounds for the West Indies fish and a pound, five shillings for the rest, which is really no better than tomcod."

"Thirty-four pounds? Thirty-four poun', five shillin' fer one year of work?" Theophilous turned red above his beard.

"More than it's worth, I'm afraid. The price of fish is down everywhere, and our profit margin is dangerously thin. But I'm willing to charge more to your account, Theophilous. Now let's see, how much is it you owe me?"

"And well enough ya know!" snarled Theo.

"Let's just look in the book, shall we?" The clerk pushed over the leatherbound book with its columns of figures only the merchants understood.

"Why, look at this," he said, as if surprised. "You owe one hundred pounds, ten shillings. That's quite a large sum. Been living a bit high, perhaps, spending money on foolish luxuries, buying all that twine and those hooks last year, maybe more flour than you could use? But that's none of my affair. You made your decisions and you must live with them.

"In any event, Theophilous, and of course you are welcome to check my figures" —as if he did not know that Theo could not read— "you owe me eighty-six pounds, five shillings. Now, how do you propose to pay this great amount? Or am I expected to offer you credit once again?"

Theophilous gritted his teeth. "You knows ever'thin' I got is in them piles of fish—and good fish it is!"

Then the rich boy spoke, languidly, as if requesting another tea cookie.

"Cut them off," said Edmund Treadwell.

To be cut off? No credit for supplies? How could they make it through the winter? But the fat rich boy went on.

"These people plainly do not understand hard work. If they choose to be lazy or improvident, that is not our concern. If we reward the weak, why should the rest work? Those who pay their bills will be given credit, within reason. Those who have not earned enough should be cut off."

Then he said six words that branded themselves into Tom's brain.

"And those who starve, deserve it."

Tom took a deep breath, but the elder merchant, who had at least grown up here and knew the people, said,

"Now, now, Master Edmund, the Good Book requires we stewards of trust to be merciful. Perhaps I am being over-generous, but still I think we might carry the Piccots on our books for one more year."

Edmund Treadwell sniffed his fingers and shrugged. "If you think it wise to be so generous."

Theophilous exploded but kept talking to the man he knew, addressing his words to Merchant Simons. "Generous! 'Tis nothing 'generous' about it! You knows as soon as we'm out of sight, you'll barrel up me fish, call it all mer-chantable, and sell it High Grade, after paying us Low!"

Edmund started to sit up, but Merchant Simons motioned him back.

"My business practices are not your concern. And we have other fishermen waiting. My offer is a fair one, and I have made it. If you want your supplies, sign here and take the credit slip. Go on board the ship, collect your goods.

"Or, if you prefer, take your fish elsewhere."

They both knew Theophilous had nowhere else to go. Even if he had a way to transport all his dried fish to St. John's, there was no competition there. The merchants all knew each other and paid the same low price.

Theo stood motionless for a long moment. Then his broad shoulders slumped. He took the quill pen out of the ink and scratched a black X on the book beside his name.

Tom felt a wave of helpless rage. These men were pulling them down, stealing the hard work of their lives, like the kraken had snatched away his halibut. He glared at the boy who would so casually sentence them to starve.

Edmund saw, looked back, and because he was after all a boy himself, lifted his eyebrows as if to say, what are you going to do about it? Tom hesitated, not wanting to get his family in trouble. Then Edmund smiled, and the mockery in those sneering lips was more than Tom could take.

Words burst out, all unplanned. "You great thievin' pig, who is you to say me family should starve?"

It was suddenly very quiet. Even outdoors things seemed to stand still. Tom had said out loud what all the fishermen thought.

"*Pig*, did you say, you outport scum fisherboy?" Edmund was suddenly standing, languid attitude forgotten. His shoulders bulged beneath his shirt.

"Hush, Tom!" snapped Theo.

"I'm thinkin' the boy will apologize," said the merchant, for a moment forgetting his phony English accent. "We're merchants, businessmen, not to be called thieves. Ye owe us everything: yeer clothes, yeer food, yeer very lives. I'm thinkin' the boy will apologize. Now."

"I won't," said Tom, though a shudder ripped up his stomach muscles.

"A question of honor," said Edmund, "that seems to demand an immediate answer."

"What'll ya do, hit me wi' yer lacy hankecher'?" said Tom. He had never used a handkerchief himself, but he had heard about them and figured Edmund was the sort of person to own one.

"No. I will just . . . thrash you," said Edmund, taking a pair of thin black gloves out of his pocket. As he snugged them on, a faint bulge showed at the knuckles. No one else knew about the thin strips of metal inside, converting a pair of gentlemen's gloves into what thugs called knuckledusters.

When the larger youth put up his fists and took a strange-looking step toward him, Tom had no idea what was going on. Boxing was an English sport, unknown in Newfoundland. Tom could hold his own in a scuffle, of course—wrestle and punch, shake hands afterward—but to plan and rehearse the destruction of a human being? That was not Tom. Aside from the occasional short flare of temper, he had no wish to harm anyone.

"No need fer this!" Theo put in quickly.

"Of course not. Your son will apologize," said Simons.

Theo looked at Tom, who was still glaring at Edmund. "Don't step on the fish." Theophilous sighed.

"Oh, my, yes, be careful of the fish!" said the merchant, for once in complete agreement with Theo.

Tom backed up a bit, clear of the stacks of dried cod. The larger boy followed, both hands high before his face. So smug he looked, as though he had won already.

Tom lunged in quickly. He had a favorite trick that often won him scuffles outright. If he hooked his left heel behind his opponent's and slammed him with both stiffened palms, he could knock him down and fall right on top, thumping out the loser's wind. Then he would step back and wait until the other recovered, after which they would talk and go about their business.

But not this time. As Tom came forward, Edmund's right fist crashed into Tom's forehead. The knuckle-duster gloves, backed by 180 pounds of mostly muscle, knocked Tom back as if he'd run into a wall.

He staggered and stepped, dodging to gain time, but his moves were slow. He was dizzied, blinking.

Edmund followed with a lunging left jab, slower than the punch before.

Tom stepped to the right to get out of the way.

The heavy, slamming right cross came. The punch went right through Tom's blocking hands to land squarely on his nose.

Tom felt the planks of the store underneath him. Then

Edmund was standing over him.

Tom put up his hand to wipe his face. His fingers came away red.

"You're too easy," said Edmund.

Tom threw his weight backward into a roll, coming up quick, staggering, but on his feet.

Edmund advanced in that odd mincing shuffle. Tom dived at the bigger boy's legs. Maybe if he could tackle him, get him on the ground—

Something like an ax handle crashed on his left cheek just below the eye. He stumbled and went to his knees. A hooking left slammed his right ear.

Tom heard a roaring as his brain shook in his skull. Then the last punch came.

Darkness closed around him.

CHAPTER FIVE

THE LAST DAY OF SCHOOL . . . AND WHY MOM HATED DOGS

◆ ◆ ◆

As if from underwater, Tom struggled toward consciousness. He saw his mother's face, the lines across her forehead deepening—Ma's getting old, he realized suddenly—then Murphy's huge and hairy face came near, and his mother pulled away quickly. The dog's long pink tongue swabbed his face, reviving him with warmth and slobber.

"Murphy, don't do that," he said, and somewhere far away he thought he heard his mother crying.

"B'y?" said Theophilous, brown face looking tough enough to sand wood, but his voice more gentle than Tom remembered. "B'y, speak yer name. Do ya know who ya are?"

It was the oddest thing. Tom knew who he was, but as

for the exact name he went by, that seemed to have slipped away. "Don't be tarmentin' me wi' such as that," he said, to cover his confusion.

Tom remembered how he had come to be lying on the wooden planks of the store. He sat up, but too quickly, and the sudden motion made his head seem to roll. He turned, put his hands down, and threw up on the floor. He paused a second, then tried again. He made it to his feet, but the floor seemed very far away now, and it swayed. He still didn't know who he was.

"Are ya all right, Tom?" Tom. There it was, easy as that. Somebody already knew his name, they should have just asked . . . her, 'stead of botherin'.

"Tom. That's me name," he said, and the words came strangely, as if his mind and mouth were a great distance apart. He was not even entirely sure if it was himself who had answered when Rosie's face swam into focus.

Rosie. Oh, no. She was here, too? He didn't want her to see him like this, all weakish and sick. "I'm fine, lass. Just a bit dizzy, is all."

Other faces crowded near, and he heard voices, too fast and too many to know who was who.

"Should have seen yer dog."

"Like a thunderbolt 'e was."

"Thought 'e'd tear that big boy's throat out."

"Ahrr, 'e were some surprised, that Edmund Treadwell was, to find hisself knocked down and a hunnert-odd pounds o' dog on his chest!"

"What did Murphy do?" asked Tom.

"Didn't hurt him none, just a warnin' like. But 'e had fat boy's throat all snug in his mouth. Left little tooth marks when 'e finally let go, and growled and come over to stand 'longside of you. Thought we'd have to shoot 'im just to let us get near," said Daniel Squires.

"Nobody's shootin' me dog," said Tom, looking into Murphy's small red eyes. Murphy panted, pink tongue lolling out, and looked at Tom with such affection and concern, as if the boy was the pet and Murphy the owner.

"'E's a good dog, that. The merchant was fer shootin' 'im, but we'd not stand fer it."

"Where's—what's his name?"

"Oh, aye, the owner's brat. 'E's gone to change his pertty clothes."

Cold sweat popped from Tom's forehead. His eyes did not seem to be working together, so the people on his right and left sides faded in and out independently of each other.

The walk home seemed very long, especially up the hill, and his end of the handled sledge felt very light, as though there was nothing on it.

People tried to steer him all the time. "No, Tom, don't turn that way, careful now, b'y," the voices kept saying. And besides, where were their supplies? he wondered. Hadn't they gone for supplies?

When he got home he found himself going to bed, which was very strange because it was only the middle of the day. Then everything went away for a while.

When he woke next, he looked down at his hands sticking out of the bed covers and twitched his fingers. They still obeyed him, but jerkily, as if he'd drunk too much tea and had the nervousness.

He heard the sound of a needle pushing through cloth. His eyes moved, though not his head. He didn't want to move his head just yet.

His mother had brought a chair and her sewing, and was quietly doing her work beside him. It's odd, Tom thought, when she sews, it's sewin'. But when me dad sews a net, that ain't sewin', that's workin' on the net. But it is still sewin'. How come when a man and a woman does sewin', they calls it by different names? The thought faded.

He studied his mother a moment. Good old Ma. Skinny and tall, gray hair, glasses she used for close work slowly falling down her nose.

They didn't fit her, having been willed her from a big-nosed neighbor who'd died. The glasses gave her a headache, she told him once, but they made things look bigger, and that was good. Ma edged up her glasses with a practiced twitch of her face and saw Tom was awake. She smiled.

"Ma?" said Tom.

"Hmm?"

"How come you hates dogs so much?"

She frowned and for a moment actually stopped work. Then, as if deciding something deep within herself, she nodded. "All right," she said, and put the needle carefully aside.

Then she undid the button on her right sleeve and rolled it up.

Tom saw the heavy scarring on her wrist and forearm. He had noticed it before, when she was doing dishes.

"You mind how I told you I got this?" said Ma.

"Yis, a burn, from when you was a little girl," said Tom, and a chill ran suddenly up his spine so that he shivered for no reason.

"That wasn' true. It was a make-up story, which I told you so as not to give you me own fear. Dogs done it. I was just a girl then, gettin' water from the brook. It was in the starvin' time, ever'body thin and near the edge. People holdin' out best they could, tryin' to make it till the fish come back. Vegetables gone. Root cellar empty. Nobody had extra fer no dog. We was starvin', and the dogs, they was starvin', too.

"Anyway, I had me yoke and buckets to get the water—for me ma didn't have no boys—and a whole bunch o' dogs come betwixt me and the path to the house. They kinda walked around me fer a bit, and then one nipped me on the ankle, and t' other knocked me down, grabbed onta me arm, growlin'. I was yellin' fer me dad, which was foolish on account of he was off in the boat. But I wasn' idle, o' course. I had the carry-yoke betwixt the buckets, see, and was usin' that to keep 'em off me throat. But they was too many.

"They'd killed me certain if not fer yer grandfather workin' at the woodpile. He heard me yellin' and come to help."

Marian Piccot clucked her tongue.

"Look at me, an idle gossip, chattin' like I've nothin' to do." She took up her sewing again. "Anyhow, I never cared fer dogs much since then."

"Murphy's not like that," said Tom. He sat up quickly, which made his head spin.

"I know," she said.

"I better go feed him," said Tom, making to get out of bed.

"I already done it," said Ma.

Thus did Murphy become family.

The clipper ship went north along the coast to other outport villages to get their catch and take it to St. John's. Edmund went with it.

But his image did not leave Tom's mind. Every day he remembered the one-sided battle, refought it in his mind. He felt shamed in front of everyone.

And one night, as he sat in the twine loft helping Theo and Daniel make a new leaf of fishnet, Tom tried to put his feelings into words. "I can't let 'er loose," he said as he filled another eight-inch wooden net needle with twine. This one he set beside his father. The round-ended needle Theo held was almost empty.

"Meanin' what?" grunted Theo, tying off another four-inch square of the net. There were ninety-nine squares, or meshes, to each drew, which was one line of the leaf, which was one section of the net. The two older men worked on the net while Tom filled the needles. The completed portion of the leaf hung on the wall in front of them.

"I got to beat 'im somehow." Tom started filling the next needle right away, wrapping twine through the narrow slot and around both ends. Net needles only carried the string. They did not poke holes in anything.

"Ya wants to fight the merchant's son again?"

"I do," said Tom. "Feels like I has to."

The twine loft was roomy, filling most of the second story of the Piccots' house. It was a good place for men to work with their hands while their bodies rested. The mixture of smells was comforting, pleasant: the pungent stink of tar and chewing tobacco was gentled by the good wood smells of spruce, cedar, birch, pine, and the ever-present nearness of the sea. It was also warm in the net loft, but from need, not luxury. The mud and stone fireplace used a lot of wood (which Tom knew very well, he being the one who fed it), but men could not work their hands clever on the nets if fingers were stiff with the cold.

Murphy curled at Tom's feet. It was not normal for a dog to be allowed in the net loft, but his defense of Tom had raised his status, and he was now allowed inside.

"Won't do," said Theo.

"Why not?" asked Tom.

"That boy, what's his name? Edmund? 'E's too big. More like a man nor a boy. I shoulda stopped it meself. That weren't a fight, more like a slaughterin'."

"I'll do better next time!" said Tom.

"How? 'E outweighs you fifty poun'. Be sensible. Some things ya just got to accept. Like how the merchants is wi' us. And ya mind when that big squid o' yours took yer halibut? Nothin' ya could do 'bout it."

Tom considered. In his memory the squid loomed huge and impossible to fight.

"I mind me a little feller *almost* whupped a big guy once in a fight over in St. John's," said Daniel Squires. "Mainland feller, 'e was, Frenchy somethin'-or-other. Nice man, aside from 'e talked peculiar."

"How'd 'e do his fightin'?" asked Tom.

"Strangest thing," said Daniel. "Wi' his feet."

"Nohow!" said Tom.

"That 'tis, b'y," said Daniel, meaning he was absolutely serious. "I'm tellin' ya true, not cufferin' at all this time.

"I asked him how 'e done that wi' his feet, and Frenchy said ya had to keep yer balance, and practice. Oh, but ya know what 'e said was the most important thing? 'E said ya had to do this kind o' *stretchin'* thing. I can't do 'er, but I mind how 'e did—look."

Daniel set down the section of new net and cleared a space on the floor.

Then he sat with his legs straight out, wide apart as they would go. He leaned forward, or tried to, grunting, hardly moving forward at all.

"These here guywires got to be loose," he said, touching the muscles on the inside of his thigh. "If they're loose, 'e says, ye can kick higher than a growed man's head."

Tom had to try it, of course, sitting down on the hard board flooring, putting his feet way out wide. He leaned forward. Pain shot along the inside of his thigh. Even his young muscles were too tight. "Whoa!" he said. "This stretchin' business don't feel good."

"Frenchy said ya has to do that ever' day."

"I don't need that. Let me just try kickin' straight up."

Standing straight, Tom kicked at an imaginary Edward six feet up from the decking. But his legs were too tight for such a kick, and the foot went only about four feet off the floor. He staggered, almost fell.

"Let me try that stretchin' bit again." Tom sat down and put his legs wide. This time he got a little bit farther. When he stood up and kicked again, the result was slightly better.

"If you'm through fightin' wi' the air," said Theo, "ya might try windin' me some twine."

"Yis, b'y," said Tom, picking up the work again.

He was quiet for a moment, perhaps even two. Then he remembered. "But, Dan'l, you said Frenchy *almost* won the fight."

"Yis, b'y, 'e got too clever one time, and this cook 'e was fightin', 'e got a hold of Frenchy's leg. Throwed him right down and sot on him. We broke it up after that. They was both lookin' frazzled to a snot."

Silence for a while, then, "I mistrusts them gloves Edward put on his hand," Tom said. "Feeled like getting hit wi' a rock."

"Oh, ahrr, they're a weapon, sure enough," said Daniel.

The winds outside rushed louder, swaying the building so it creaked and groaned. In winter the winds had more substance, the air being thicker, squeezed together by the cold, and it shook the houses on their wood foundations.

"Gettin' cold, Skipper," said Tom.

"I knows, b'y." His father nodded.

"Chamber pot froze over this mornin'."

There were no toilets in those days. People either went outside and found a private place, or used the chamber pot. At the stage the men used the trunk hole over the sea, and the sculpins swimming underneath disposed of the nuisance.

"Winter'll be early this year, no question," said Theo. "Matter o' fact, no sense you startin' off to the school. I'll be needin' ya for the wood," he added, to Tom's astonishment and delight. "Soon as the ground's hard enough, we're goin' to take the country path, put that play-toy animal o' yours to work along wi' the three dogs what Dan'l's already gathered."

"I'm goin' to the country!" said Tom.

"Yis, b'y," said Daniel.

"'Tis wonnerful fine!" said Tom.

"May not be so fine when the blizzard hits, hey Dan'l?" said Theo.

"It gets cold out there, for certain," said Daniel, "not snug and warm like in t' cove. I mind me one time it got so cold the fire froze. Had to thaw out the flames afore they would light."

Tom thought for a moment. "You 'lows that can't be true," he said.

"Why, that ain't nothin', b'y, I remembers—"

Then, through the wind outside there came a high, thin scream, wild and clear and thrilling.

"It's them! The eiders is come!" Tom raced to the window on the twin loft's north side. "The eiders always brings the first blizzard, Grandpa says—I mean, he used to say." He could not see the eider ducks through the fat flakes of snow, but he could hear them.

"Almost time to be goin'," said Theophilous. He breathed

a long, slow inhalation, as if to draw in all the comfort of the room they would soon have to leave. "We'll wait till the blizzard blows over and the ground gets firm. Can't walk on no marshes nor ponds till they freezes. But you'd best make yer excuses to the new schoolteacher. Oh, and split a bunch more wood fer your ma."

Three days later the snowstorm eased, though large flakes continued to fall. The men took the big flakes to mean that the blizzard was pretty much over. "The smaller the snow, the bigger the blow" the old saying went.

Tom could not get to school fast enough for the joy of saying good-bye.

He hurried Mark Josephus into his clothes, and then stuffed down the baked salt-cod breakfast quick as he could. Even so, Mark Josephus was ready before him, with two chunks of chopped wood in his arms.

"Attaboy, Mark, ya got the junks fer the teacher already," said Tom.

"Baby Sally is too young to go to school," Mark Josephus said smugly, hugging the wood to his jacket.

"That's true, b'y, she's not all big like you," agreed Tom.

Then they were on their way.

"Mornin', Peggeen, I mean Miz' Peggeen," said Tom as they entered the schoolroom, which on Sundays was the church. When the bedroom doors were open, it was also a lodge for important visitors.

"Hello, Tom!" she said, her round red face warm and glowing, friendly as a stove. "My goodness, Mark Josephus, you are getting so big!"

"Baby Sally's too small to come to school," Mark said, twisting his chunky body halfway round and back again, "and *I* was the one who remembered the wood."

"Well, good for you. I appreciate that!"

Almost bursting with his secret, Tom went to his usual place, standing by the wall. There were no desks except the teacher's. The students stood all day at the edges of the classroom, where flat boards stuck out waist-high from the wall. Each board had a black slate and some hard chalk, also a rag to moisten for erasures. The girls brought small wooden water containers. The boys mostly did not bother with this, favoring a more natural source of supply.

"Miz' Peggeen, ma'am?"

"Yes, Tom?" asked Peggeen.

"Today is me last day," said Tom.

"Oh, no. Why?" Peggeen seemed upset.

"I'm too old fer schoolin' now. I got to be goin' to the woods. Me family needs me helpin'."

"Let's talk outside," said Peggeen. "Students, copy your alphabet, capital letters all the way through. Those who know how, help the ones who don't. I'll be right back."

The scratch of hard chalk on the slates mingled with groans at the busywork. Tom and Peggeen stepped out on new snow.

"Tom, I know you don't love school."

Tom snorted. "That's fer true!"

"But school is about your whole future, and—and our country's future! I won't let you throw it away without a fight."

Tom said nothing.

"Talk, come on, talk about it. This might be our last chance!" she said.

Tom looked at her earnest face.

"I don't want to hurt yer feelin's none, Peggeen. But I pure hates school. Not just old Whipper Treadwell, though he were a waste of flesh, fer certain. But truth is, I can't see what good this stuff does—I mean why should I go on readin' the Royal Reader book, like that poem about Mary and her stupid little goat?"

"Lamb," corrected Peggeen automatically.

"Well, whatever she had, them mainland animals ain't no nevermind to me. But why should I know about readin'? I'll be a fisherman. The ocean's me book."

"Oh, Tom, Tom! The Royal Readers are just how you get started, but writing itself, words—words are like *worlds,* life itself all scrunched down into print. Once something is wrote down, the man who wrote it could be dead, but still he talks to you! Once you have the skill, you can do anything you want with it! And our country, we—why do the merchants get away with robbin' us the way they do? Because almost none of us can read or write! We can't even know what the numbers in their account books mean!"

"That's just—how it is," said Tom.

"Just because something is doesn't mean 'tis right! Look, I just finished this wonderful—wait here!" Peggeen dashed into the schoolroom and rushed back before Tom quite realized she was gone. She pushed something heavy into his hands.

It was a book. Tom turned it to the pale wintry light. A snowflake fell on the leather cover with its inscribed picture of a strong, tall boy, ax in hand, chopping some splits for the fire. Behind him rose a sturdy little house, like a tilt you would build in the woods.

Tom studied the lettering carefully.

"*Life of Ab-ra-ham Lin-coll-in,*" he said.

"You say it like Ling-kun," said Peggeen.

"'Tis a fine thing," said Tom. Aside from the Royal Readers, he had seen two books before, both Bibles. One was in the church, the other in his home.

"Read it," said Peggeen.

"Well, I ain't got the time right now, and I'd be scared to borrow it, and—"

"It's yours."

"Mine? You're givin' me a whole book?"

"Yes, and you'd better take care of it, or I'll rip the hair off your head."

Tom was suddenly afraid to hold it. An actual book. It had a leather cover on it, and—

"You take it to the woods with you, and you read some every day, you promise?" She stepped forward, crowding his space.

"I might get 'er wet," said Tom weakly.

"Wrap it in oilcloth," said Peggeen.

Time dragged. The old-timers said the marshes were not firm enough to cross; the ice had to thicken on the peatlands, heath, and lakes and ponds of the Avalon Peninsula. Could fall through the ice, did you go too early.

The work of fall went on. Nearby dead trees had to be chopped and dragged in for the winter's fires. Fishing nets had to be barked, which meant boiling a big pot of water containing spruce tops, salt water, and tar. When the liquid in the pot was dark and thick enough, nets were lowered into it, one by one, and left an hour before being hung out to dry. Barking preserved the nets, protecting them for the long months of storage ahead. They might even be barked once more before summer fishing began.

Ma cooked spruce tops, too, only with fresh water and without tar, mixing in molasses for a good-tasting drink called switchel. Switchel was not only a pleasure, but, like fruit, kept the scurvy sickness away.

Ma also mixed some vinegar with baking soda to make a drink that bubbled and boiled like a storm in the kettle.

But when it was done, the drink had a strong, sharp taste that would really wake you up.

Some of the fishermen made seines, long nets with very small meshes, the net-holes so small even the smallest fish could not escape.

Theo did not approve of this. He threw little ones back, and his nets had larger mesh so that immature fish could get away. "Kill the little fish today, ye'll have no big uns tomarrow'" was his belief. "'Tis foolish, like a man burnin' down his own house to keep his ownself warm."

The wind turned bitter harsh and found its way indoors, rippling the floor-covering canvas under the family's feet. Sailcloth made good carpet, being easy to keep clean. Just go over to Beachy Cove where there was some sand and toss that down, then broom it out and the floor was clean. (If you wanted to get real fancy, you would make a design in the sand on the canvas and leave it for the people to admire one second before they walked on it. Such short-lived designs were called the Walls of Jericho after the Bible story of the walls that fell at the blast of a trumpet.) It was fun when the floor rippled under your feet, like standing on a sail.

The time for fishing was mostly over now except for those rich enough (it cost forty shillings!) to buy a berth for the winter fishery over to the Labrador, seventeen miles of ocean away. Theophilous had a gun and could have gotten a free berth as a gunner on a sealing ship, but he did not have enough powder to shoot with, and in any event his dad had always warned him to "steer clear of swilin'," which was the risk-laden business of sealing.

Theo had taken young Tom to the graveyard one day and pointed to the grass-covered headstone of a sealing skipper. "He was after swilin' all his life till he froze the fingers off both hands. He died owin' money, same as we. To go out on the ice after seals, sure, 'tis excitin', but best to stick to the fishin' we knows."

There was another, darker reason for not going on the sealing ships. It was a reason Theo knew and Tom did not, and it was the reason for the name of Piccot's Gulch, a narrow canyonlike rift to the sea just along the coast a ways. But of this Theo said nothing, and Daniel kept the secret as well, feeling it not his to give.

While they waited for the time to be right for leaving, Ma made trigger mitts for Tom and Theo. These gloves had a thumb, and a finger, and the other three fingers in one, so they'd have some use of the digits but the fingers would still be warm.

Tom, Theo, and Daniel filled up new racquets, weaving twine across the paddle-shaped frames to make snowshoes. The backpacks were heavy with what food there was. Ma sewed a hood onto an old jacket of Grandfather's and made Tom a chestpad. This was a piece of blanket with armholes to wear snug beneath the jacket and overtop his long underwear.

The snow built up, thawed, and hardened. Another layer fell, building on the first. Tom thought they would never get going.

Some days he stared out at the icy waters of the cove, especially out toward Oar's Deep, where he'd seen the squid. He wondered if the kraken visited the cove by night. Maybe it was out there right now. Waiting.

Other days he spent time working with Murphy, putting the leather-strap harness on him but without the slide attached, just getting the big dog used to the feel.

Today was another training day. Murphy growled once, low and threatening in his chest, but Tom reached under, chucked his jaw together, and said sharply, "No!" and Murphy blinked.

Tom sat down beside him with the harness touching them both. "This ain't goin' to hurt you none. But I does need yer help," he said.

Murphy nudged the harness. Sniffed it. Looked at Tom.

"I know, it smells awful from the tar, but we can't have you eatin' it, see?"

Murphy seemed to sigh. After a while Tom put on the straps. Tom loved him up good, praising him and scratching his back and his head, and Murphy let it happen.

A couple more days of the dog wearing the straps, and Tom took the slide out and tied Murphy to it. Then he walked off and called Murphy—who followed.

After that it was no problem to climb on the slide and throw a snowball at Murphy, yell "Oo-eesht!" to start, and just watch the muscles surge beneath the black-haired coat. Tom taught Murphy the simple vocabulary of sled dogs— "Haul in" to turn left, "Keep off" to turn right, "Attaboy" to go faster, and "Aa, Aa!" to stop.

Tom was a little worried about what would happen when Murphy met the other three dogs recently acquired by Daniel Squires. Would they fight?

Murphy was lying on his paws in the snow when the other three arrived already in the harness, ready to practice. Tom was watching him close, and he saw the red eyes open and then close again when the three were coming up the path. Ahab, the dominant animal, was a blue-eyed malamute. He strutted over close to Murphy, who continued to lie there as if asleep.

But when Ahab peeled his lip, ruffled up his neck hair, and gave a short exploratory growl, Murphy opened one eye and looked straight at him. And then closed the eye again.

Ahab let his ruffling neck hair smooth.

Thus simply was it settled. Without fuss or fighting at all.

When Tom put the dogs in harness, one after the other, Murphy stepped into line behind Ahab.

At last the great day came. Leaving!

"Bye, Baby Sally. Bye, Mark Josephus. You study hard in school, now!"

"Bring me a fur!" commanded Baby Sally.

"A water bear!" said Mark Josephus.

"How 'bout you, Lynny?" said Tom, grinning at his older sister as she hugged him good-bye. "What shall I bring you?"

"Just—come home safe—ye goat-chin boy!" she said, pinching his jaw with its nearly transparent whiskers just beginning to sprout. Tom rubbed his chin. "I'll be growin' me a beard just to scratch yer cheek!" He wondered idly what it would be like if he had a beard and kissed a girl.

The dogs were hitched up, two by two: Murphy and Ahab up front; then Skinner and Charley, the two black Labradors at the back; and the slide behind them. The men would be walking until they got out on smooth snow with a good slick crust. Then the sled would slide easily, and they could take turns riding on the heels, the butt end of the sled runners.

Tom had on his new snowshoes and was shifting his weight experimentally, getting used to the equipment. He had been walking on wide snow racquets every winter since he was old enough to walk, and he knew the stiffish, leaning walk without having to think about it.

He hugged his ma, and she clutched him too tight for a second, as if afeared to let him go. "I'll just be gone a few days, Ma," he said, embarrassed to be hugged in front of others. She let go of him, patted his shoulder awkwardly, turned away quickly, and went inside.

Tom looked around the snowed-in village, seeking a certain missing somebody. But the windows of Rosie's house showed nothing. She should be out and doing her chores. Oh, there! The door to the Crandall's house opened up, and his heart seemed to stop. His head lifted, then sagged. It was just Widow Crandall, tossing the leftover breakfast to their dogs. Rosie almost always was the one did this, and when Tom was out doing wood or water, they'd run over and talk for a bit. Why wasn't she there now, today? Was she sick? Was something wrong?

"Don't stand there gawkin', b'y," said Theo.

Suddenly the excitement of the moment filled Tom, and he was eager to be on the way.

"Ooo-eesht, now! Attaboy!" yelled Theo to the dogs, and Daniel threw a snowball at Ahab just to get them started.

They walked slowly up the steep grade, following the streamside path. When they reached the top, where The Barrens began, Tom turned and looked back at his home waters of Portugal Cove and Conception Bay.

To the right of Bell Island, out in the bay, he saw a tall iceberg on its way in. The island of ice was much bigger than a ship. Around it in the cove were small blue disks of pancake ice, not thick enough yet for boys' feet to jump on. The water was far too cold for swimming, but that didn't seem to stop anyone. "Copying" was a favorite delight, leaping from icepan to icepan, and it didn't count with big chunks large enough to take your weight. You had to keep going fast, leaping from ice to ice quickly, or sink. As many of the boys could not swim, it was an exciting pastime, but best done in shallow water. Flecks of white— eider ducks—rose and fell with the waves.

Tom saw his own house. He could see no one moving.

Everybody must be inside, going about their business. It made him somehow sad to think that life went on without him.

Well! There were adventures waiting!

"We're goin' down north, we're goin' down north," sang Tom to himself, though in one sense they were headed toward the top of the world and might easily be said to be going up. But Newfoundlanders figured going north was heading in to the center of the world, and so they said they were headed down north.

Tom looked across the white wastes of The Barrens, spotted here and there with small stands of logged-over growth: larch and spruce, pine, cedar, birch and fir—cut down before and not yet grown back enough to be re-harvested. Aside from the low clumps of trees, everything looked pretty much the same. It was hard to tell the difference between peatland and bog, ponds and solid ground.

"How do we—not get lost?" he asked. "How do we know where we're goin'?"

"What?" said Daniel Squires. "I thought *you* was the one knowed the way!"

Tom grinned. "No, fer true."

"Well, we kinda do and kinda don't. We knows some of the way off by heart, o' course. The handy woods, what is nearby, that's family. We wouldn't bother the Andersons' little woods, nor he take ours, such as we needs for cook fires and the like. But fer the virgin woods, them as is untouched? Well, we has a general idea where that is. Good day's travel, 'cept if we runs into a starm. If the trees we comes to is too small or somebody else has cut over 'em, we just keeps goin'. We been this way before, and so has the animals.

"We'm on a caribou path right now. Looky there, where

the snow's blowed thin and there's scratches in the ground? Them's deer paths, caribou feet dug 'em out. They goes the same way ever' year. P'rhaps we'll meet 'em, get us some country meat!

"And ya notice how yer father's walkin' backward just now? That's good habit fer the woods, knowin' how the country looks goin' t'other way, fer the return trip."

Tom turned around and walked backward for a bit. It did look different this way. He tried to fix the scene in his mind in case he'd have to walk home by himself.

Theo said nothing.

They walked in silence for a long while, feet crunching the snow. Their breaths made steam in the morning air.

Tom was not one to be quiet for long, and when he judged Theo had been walking long enough to be fully awake and in a reasonably good mood, he began the conversation again.

"Might we see white bears?" Tom asked.

"Not likely," said Theo.

"They sometimes walks over from the mainland," said Daniel, "when the ice freezes hard."

"Oh, ahrr, 'tis not far to the mainland. Sometimes they does come over when it freezes up, or maybe rides on a bit of ice. 'Course yer white bear swims pretty good anyhow, that's why we calls un the water bear."

"Could we shoot un?"

"If we still got ammunition left. I only got three shots, not even a blank shot to clean out me barrel," said Theo. "Cost too much powder to bury Grandfather. I almost didn't bring me gun at all 'cept we might get us a deer. I washed 'er barrel out good as I could with water, run a cloth down 'er throat and that, but still I'd like to have got off that one clean-out shot, just to be sure the barrel don't blow."

"Couldn't ya git more powder from the merchant?"

"After yer little mix-up with the fat boy? We got what we got, and that's all. I sold 'em the fish, and we kept the cullage—what they calls the cullage—to eat our ownselves over the winter. But there'll be no more credit till we pays our bill. As if we can, much as they charges fer ever'thin', and little as they pays fer our fish." Theophilous was frowning again.

Tom changed the subject. "What else could we meet—woodsdevil, p'rhaps?" A chill of excitement shot up Tom's spine as he named the creature often talked of by his school yard friends, but which none of them had seen.

"Don't be speakin' on them evil craytures," said Theo. "Bad luck. Might bring 'em near."

"They's scarce anyhow," put in Dan'l to soothe things over.

"And we wants to keep it like that," snapped Theo.

Tom said nothing more for a while, but he scanned every shadow, every footprint in the snow, searching for the devil of the woods.

CHAPTER SIX

"WHY WE KILLS . . ."

◆   ◆   ◆

They slept the first night in a lean-to—one small spruce laid across the forks of two trees close together, and six smaller chopped trees leaning up against that.

Tom built the fire. First, to make rinds, he found a pollard, a birch tree with the bark peeled off (and therefore dead). Then, breaking off a dry limb, Tom whittled a fergee. The fergee looked like a wooden porcupine, a mass of still-attached splinters at one end: it was the fire starter. A scrap of dry cloth (rag saved for tinder), and the sparks from a piece of file hammered on by a fire ax (a tiny chip of flint tied to a little handle), and a red dot glowed. Presently a tiny flame grew under Tom's breath, warming his face as the fergee caught. The prebuilt structure of wood chunks lit from that. They had a fire.

In separate blankets and wearing all their clothes, the three slept in the lean-to with the fire going into the night. They did not sleep warm, but they slept, only occasionally shivering themselves awake and throwing more wood on the fire.

The dogs curled up and let the snow blow over them. The dogs did not shiver.

Morning came early.

Tom was deep in an embarrassing dream, warm and intense, so private that its secrets would never be shared, especially not with one certain girl, a central figure in the dream.

Viselike fingers clutched his shoulder.

"Time, b'y. Up and about," Theo ordered.

As he rolled out from under the covers, the morning wind struck cold. It was still dark. Tom could make out the bulky forms of the winter-clad men as they knelt by the dogs, adjusting a chest-strap here, checking a footpad there.

Shivering, clumsy with cold and sleep, Tom stumbled to the edge of the clearing. Fumbling through layers of clothing, he stood wide-legged and let loose the night's water. Must be nice to be a dog sometimes, he thought, just have to lift a leg. Oh, well, least he wasn't a woman, have to go hide all the time. Men could just go where they was, pretty much.

His nuisance gotten rid of, Tom scuffled his hands through clean snow, brushed off the ice crystals, and slipped on his warm woolen mitts again. He was awake.

Let's see, chores, uhh . . .

"Feed 'em in harness today, b'y, we wants 'em used to workin' together," said Theo.

Dim light slowly filtered in from overhead, but Tom

could not see the sun nor feel its heat. He shivered as he opened the dogs' grub box. The fish inside were frozen. He used the hand ax to break them apart.

Daniel found a coal with possibilities and blew on it. Presently they had a fire again, and they cooked the fish— well, thawed them.

Being fed, the dogs seemed like wolves, gulping the fish and looking for more. Tom gave each of them three fish and closed the grub box firmly. They had brought as much food for the dogs as they could carry, mostly conners, small bony fish with no market value. He hoped they could catch some more grub.

Tom fetched some wood. Never an end to gettin' wood, he thought, and then laughed to himself. Huh, here they were on a trip out to get wood, and what was he doin'? Gettin' wood!

When Tom got back with more branches, Daniel had snow-water warming for the tea and was mixing dough for trail bread. The recipe was not complicated: flour as much as you were hungry, water to mix, a little salt—if you had some—for flavor. The older man formed the gluey dough in a narrow white coil around the tea can's cover. The flames licked higher. Presently the bread dough began to turn golden.

Nothing smelled better than bread cooking up.

Then he remembered an unanswered question. "Quick, Uncle Dan'l, tell me about the woodsdevil! Afore Skipper gets back," he added.

"He's just an animal," said Daniel, with a glance in the direction of Theo. "A weasel, sort of, only bigger. Some folks calls un skunkbear or wolverine."

"So why is it bad luck to speak on un, if 'e's just a beast?"

"Well . . ." Daniel hesitated. "The woodsdevil—'e's different.

'E's fearful strong, fer one thing, and not skeered by any crayture nor man. I've heard tell 'e can break into a tilt, even one wi' a latched door, if ya believe that. 'E'll smash a man's gear all to wrack and ruin, eat what 'e can, stink up what 'e can't. Why they calls it skunk bear, on account of it squirts like a skunk. Whatever it stinks up, ya might as well throw away. Smart and quiet. Might be one starin' at us right now out o' them bushes."

"Is they—a *lot* o' them woodsdevils?"

"No, niver. Trappers say they is too mean. You niver sees two together 'cept I guess at matin' time, when they makes their kits. I guess they fights anythin' that comes into their country, includin' us."

Woodsdevil, thought Tom. Woodsdevil in the country, kraken in the ocean. And we in the middle.

The gloom brightened around them. Tom felt his courage growing with the light. "Shoot! I ain't worried 'bout no stinkin' skunk bear! I'd catch me a woodsdevil, if I seen un, keep un fer a play toy!"

"Well, wolverines don't make no pet. But if ya traps un, 'e's got the best fur. I seed a hood once, trimmed wi' devil's fur? Feller said that fur would never freeze, howsomever cold it got."

Then he looked over Tom's shoulder and hollered "Breakfast!" to Theo as he came tromping back.

The ice over Three Island Pond was still too thin to trust. Men and dogs took the long way around.

The land they traveled now was frozen marsh, dotted with iced-in small lakes. Sometimes they passed dome-shaped bumps—little ones being muskrat houses, the big ones beaver lodges.

In the early afternoon they came to the hill called Butterpot Dome.

"If we had time to climb it," Daniel said, "we'd see the best views in all Newfoundland, the whole Avalon Peninsula all below."

"We ain't here fer sightseein'," said Theo. They went around the hill, just high enough on its slopes to avoid the tuckamore, low growths of wind-stunted tamarack too twisted and tangled to penetrate. Sometimes the tuckamores were so thick they could be walked *on*, but not through. Under snow, of course, such a risk was not worth taking. One slip, and a broken ankle could ruin the whole voyage, taking down not only the victim but also the man who took him home.

Just ahead of them now, as they came around Butterpot Dome, was a long, slow, treeless rise.

"Over there she be," said Daniel.

Don't look like much from here, Tom thought.

When they topped the rise, he changed his mind, whistling in delight. Before and below him, far as the eye could look, rolled a sea of dark green forest: black spruce and pine, dotted here and there with stands of white birch. "Whoa! We could chop a thousand years and never run through all them trees!" said Tom.

"Don't know 'bout that," said Daniel, "but they is a lot, fer certain. See that silvery break down there? That's Manuel's River. Don't niver freeze over, hardly. Prime drinkin' water. Just walk right over, get what ya want, don't have to melt no snow. We'll build our tilt close to 'er, hey, Theo?"

Theo nodded. "But we'll log from the rise, once we has our tilt up. No sense haulin' logs farther than we has to."

They found a good flat place beside the river. Theo and Dan'l exchanged looks and nodded. They began to make their home, the tilt, or cabin, they would use while they stayed.

"We'd best hurry if we're to sleep warm," said Daniel.

They looked for spruce trees for the walls. The trees had to be a certain size—six to eight inches thick, eight to ten feet tall; and in a certain order—three tens for each eight-footer. It was fun to watch them fall.

After a tree landed, Tom hacked off the boughs while the men kept finding and felling some more, then dragging them over to Tom.

Tom kept track of where the men were cutting. Although the trees were slender from having grown in a clump close together, Tom still was not anxious to have one fall on him.

When they thought they had enough, everyone worked on the limbing. The dogs were content just to rest.

When the spruce trees were stripped, they were dragged to the clear spot down by the river. Each log was notched top and bottom at both ends. Laid foursquare on top of each other, the logs fitted notch to notch: the Indian lock. If they had had rawhide, they'd have tied the logs together. But they had not shot a caribou this year.

Now the reason for the pattern became clear: three long trees and one short. The short side left an opening. That was the door.

The walls went higher than most loggers built theirs—"I likes to be able to stand up in me tilt," Daniel said—and though Theo grumbled at this waste of time, he did not interfere, and the tilt was built taller than was needful.

While the men worked on the walls, Tom weather-proofed them, filling the cracks with moss and cold mud scooped from the river's edge. He had to do that part with his bare hands so as not to get mud on his gloves. He worked as quickly as he could, but his hands were purple when he rinsed off the mud, and they felt thick and numb and nerveless as carrots once the pain had passed. He warmed his hands in his armpits, trying to bring back some feeling.

In the afternoon he went to kill rabbits, bringing down three with his small throwing net.

When he got back, the walls were done; Tom hustled to fill in the rest of the cracks. The men brought some small trees with the limbs still on to make a temporary roof, leaving one corner open for the rock-and-mud chimney they would build.

Just before nightfall they finished.

Theo cooked inside on mud-covered stones (hill stones; river rocks might explode). Some smoke did not leave the tilt, and the men's eyes itched and burned. Still it was nice to be out of the wind.

"Tomarrow," said Daniel to Tom, "take yer tom-hawk an' dig out a trench from the fire to the wall an' underneath. Then go outside and keep diggin' 'nother couple feet. That makes an air tunnel, see? Ya cover the trench wi' rocks an' mud, leavin' it hollow inside so's ya got one end by the fire an' t'other outside. The heat o' the fire'll suck in fresh air, an' the flames'll warm it up. Chimney'll suck out the smoke better, too, you watch," said Daniel. "Then we'll be snug."

Next morning Tom built the air tunnel, and the men made a rock-and-mud chimney with a little fireplace for cooking. Once the fire started, the tilt was warm and clear of smoke, just as Daniel had said.

Theo sharpened his ax with the file. "Best keep the dogs in harness," he said. "Don't want 'em chasin' 'round, scare the fur outta the country. I'll get t' choppin' while you sets the trapline?" He raised his eyebrows at Dan'l, who nodded.

"You'll be needin' me wi' the wood, I s'pose?" asked Tom, hoping otherwise.

"Get along wi' the pair of ye," said Theo, putting an ax

across his shoulder, then heading up the ridge.

The two heard the sound of his chopping even before they had left the camp.

In packs on their backs were the precious iron traps and some rabbit meat saved from yesterday.

About half a mile from their camp, Daniel Squires found a suitable tree, a sentinel spruce, standing tall and alone, huge against gray sky.

Whittling off a piece of frozen rabbit, Daniel hung it from a branch four feet above the snow.

"Looky here," said Dan'l. Taking a trap from his backpack, he set it on the snow at the foot of the tree.

"Be mindful where ya put the traps, both 'cause we can't afford to lose 'un, an' second, 'cause ye don't want to step in 'un."

The trapline was set in a wide loop, bringing them half-circle back to camp. They had only three dozen traps. If they had a lot, say two or three hundred, they would have done like a regular trapper and built two tilts, one at each end of the line, for sleep at the end of each day. But the men were fishermen, not trappers, and besides they had tree work to do.

Tom, Dan'l, and Theo chopped and hauled trees, pausing only to limb them, working until late afternoon.

"Time fer a spell," said Theo, by which he meant not stopping but rather a change of work, a rest for the muscles by doing something different.

"Let's see what the traps got!" said Tom.

"Too early; ain't had time to do nothin' yet," said Theo.

"Tom do need to know the place, though," said Dan'l.

To which Theo made no objections.

In the first trap, the one by the sentinel spruce, was a lynx, the most beautiful cat Tom had ever seen. Its fur was a spotted cream, and its ears stood straight with tufts at the ends. Yellow eyes blazing, the cat snarled and spit at them. Helpless in the trap it stood, right foreleg broken.

"Shoot un, Skipper, quick, he's sufferin'!" said Tom.

"Can't do 'er, b'y. Would wreck the fur. Not t' mention I only got the three shots o' powder. The buryin' took too much."

Theo swung the rifle stock. Once, twice. There was a screaming snarl. Then quiet.

"I don't much like this, Skipper," said Tom.

"Like it?" growled Theo, turning suddenly, rifle looking heavy in his hands. "Think we does this 'cause we likes it?

"I ain't no St. John's feller, kill somethin' for nothin', just to leave it lay! Get it straight in yer head why we kills. We does what we must t' feed our family. Not t' mention we been cut off, remember? What happens if we don't get nothin' t' trade nor sell?

"When the starvin' time comes an' we with no food— who would be the first t' die, you reckon?"

"You mean . . ." Tom held his hand a couple feet off the snow at the height of a small child. He thought of Noddy Weathers's boy.

"Baby Sally, Mark Josephus. Little ones always goes first. That's why we does what we must t' keep t' family goin'."

Keep t' family goin' . . . Grandfather's words.

They also got a fox, but most of the traps held nothing.

The one that was farthest from the camp, however, held the frozen, bloody foot of a snowshoe hare. Theo's face tightened. Hares did not chew their feet off the way a meat-eater sometimes did.

Around the trap were strange pawprints: marks of round pads and short claws, the kind a weasel might leave if it was bigger.

"'Tis the woodsdevil, sure!" said Tom happily.

The three crouched beside the pawprints in the snow.

"Is that all the big it is?" said Tom. "Whoosh! The woodsdevil must be smaller than me dog."

Theo shook his head. "Don't matter how big 'e is. If 'e starts wreckin' our trap line . . ."

"'E could make the rounds same as we," Daniel finished for him. "Eat or ruin ever'thin', leave us wi' no fur."

"'Tis wicked!" said Tom.

"'E prob'ly thinks the same 'bout us," said Dan'l, "him bein' here first."

"Looky how the tracks goes," said Theo. "Here 'e starts off toward the next trap on the line. But now here, seems like 'e sudden changes 'is mind an' loops around."

The men exchanged glances.

"The tilt," Dan'l said.

And they were running.

CHAPTER SEVEN

THE WINTER THAT WASN'T

◆　　◆　　◆

They heard the noise first. Yapping, snarling, barking—punctuated here and there with the deep bass roar of Murphy.

"'E's fightin'!" said Tom.

"Or tryin' to," said Daniel. "They's still in harness, remember?"

The barking stopped, and the silence was somehow more frightening than the noise had been.

When the three stepped into the clearing, it seemed at first as if nothing was wrong. Murphy and the other dogs were lying down. Behind them was the doorless tilt. The dark spruce woods held silence. Whatever else had been there was now gone.

But as Murphy rose delightedly at the sight of Tom, the

tangled ropes behind him moved the slide, which was upside down. And everywhere the crusted snow was broken, marked by scrabbling feet, flattened here and there by the dragging slide.

Daniel scouted around the edges of the clearing. "Over here," he said.

Tom squatted beside him, studied the tracks, trying to guess what had happened. Here the marks of clawed feet were deep, as the wolverine stood quiet for a moment, seeing without being seen, studying the situation. The prints were clean and unblurred; he had not fidgeted. Then the tracks shallowed as he moved from concealment, right out into the open. The tracks moved back and forth with their maker in plain sight of the dogs.

"He knowed the dogs couldn't move fast, tied together like they was," said Daniel. "I think 'e was tryin' to get them dogs all worked up an' chasin', draw 'em off in the woods an' lose 'em there, an' him come back an' get our supplies."

The footprint pattern deepened again, as if the animal had stopped and listened, perhaps looked over its shoulder, sensing the approach of the humans. There was a patch of yellow in the snow, not much, as if the animal had urinated not from need but to express an opinion or to mark his territory.

And now the tracks changed altogether as the wolverine left, switching to high speed, bounding over the snow in a series of jumps, front and back feet working together in pairs. Sometimes the back feet landed in the holes in the snow the front feet had made.

"They kills caribou sometimes in the winter, runs 'em down when the deer goes slow in the snow," said Daniel.

But now the wind rose around them, and the tracks

began to fill, outlines fading under blowing snow.

"If we'd left Murphy an' them untied, they might have killed un," said Tom.

"Or been killed their ownselves," grunted Theo, heading toward the tilt.

"Good dog, Skinner! Well done, Charley! Fine dog, Ahab!" Tom said, making sure he praised each one.

But when he got to Murphy, he grabbed the dog's head and wrestled him, and the giant Newfoundland breathed in short rapid gasps, which was his way of laughing.

"Oh, I skunked Noddy Weathers fer certain!" said Tom.

"That's Noddy's dog, the one 'e said was so worthless?" asked Daniel. "I wonder do 'e got any more like *he* t' home!"

"Ain't 'e special?" said Tom.

"'E pulls 'is weight, no more'n like the others," said Theo.

Tom expressed disagreement by rubbing Murphy's ears. And the big dog lolled out his tongue and panted, completely happy in the moment.

"Can we catch un, the woodsdevil?" asked Tom as they settled in for a boilup.

"P'rhaps, wi' enough time," said Daniel Squires.

"Time we don't have," said Theo. "Dan'l, you knows this stuff best. 'Tis all up to you. Catch or kill it quick, that's all right. But if ya can't, we'll just have to bend afore the wind an' fergit the trappin' this year.

"I got me an idea," Theo continued. "I didn't want to brag on fer too much afore, fer fear bad luck comes." He glugged down half a cup of steaming tea, his throat seemingly made out of leather.

"I'm thinkin' we might git us out of debt, at least enough to git credit ag'in, keep the merchants happy, an' git our supplies."

Tom blew on his tea. He watched the ripples move over the surface like waves in a small, dark sea.

"What's the one thing no fishin' company can do without?" Theo asked.

"Fish," said Tom.

"Besides that!" snapped Theo, who was not much for joking.

"Nets an' twine?" suggested Daniel.

"Yis, but over an' above that—" Theo was getting frustrated.

"Barrels!" said Tom.

"Barrels," said Theophilous Piccot. "They got to have barrels or they can't move the fish."

"That's cooperin," said Daniel.

"We ain't coopers!" said Tom, already missing the sea.

"Ain't trappers nor yet loggers neither," said Theo, "but we does what we got to. We'll fish when summer comes, don't you worry none. But if we could do some cooperin' this winter, we might get out from the debt."

"Don't seem possible," said Daniel. "Nobody ever gets clear o' that. I figger the debt's like a mountain of stone, reachin' a'mos' up to the sky. And ivery hundred years a bird flies up to the mountain an' takes one teeny peck at the top. Now when that whole mountain gets wore down by that bird, that's when we'll pay off the debt."

"I ain't no little bird," said Theo. "And a mountain's just a big pile o' rock."

Tom looked at his father in a different way.

Theo went on. "Here's me plan. We gets more than wood fer burnin'. We gets longers fer the fish stages, short stuff fer barrel staves, an' saw-logs fer dory-buildin'.

"An' when we gets enough fer a load, somebody takes 'er home, drops 'er off to the house. No visitin', just drop off the wood, do what's needful fer the folks, an' come back.

"I figure if we drags one load a week an' don't miss no weeks, I'll have enough to start cooperin'. That's s'posin' you puts yer share in with ours, Dan'l," added Theo.

"We eats from the same flour barrel," said Daniel Squires.

"Cooperin', huh?" said Tom. His father had always been clever with wood. Boats seemed to grow almost magically under Theo's careful hands.

"People always needs barrels, that's sure enough," agreed Daniel.

"I been studyin' on it," said Theo. "Even ya merchant should want some barrels; take away from what we owes on the bill."

"Be good if we could get some iron hoop strappin' fer the barrels, maybe some nails," said Daniel. "If I can catch the woodsdevil, get us some furs, we can trade 'em."

Theo looked at Tom. "What do ya think, b'y?"

Tom was thinking of Edmund, remembering fists in black gloves.

"I'd love to put one over on that merchant's fat son," he said.

As Daniel took over the trapline, Tom and Theo worked the ridge. Chopping trees in the snow was not easy, but Tom kind of liked it. Theo kept telling Tom, "Let yer ax do the work; just swing 'er up and let 'er fall"—because Tom wasted energy, working too hard.

He loved the sound when the fibrous center of the tree tore—*crackkkshshsh*—and each fall of a tree was a blow in the fight for their lives.

They were fighting starvation with every grunt and chop, fighting the poverty that clutched their lives and tried to drag them down.

Each time they dragged a log clear of the woods, it was a little victory, a point for their side.

And every so often (when Theo wasn't looking), Tom practiced his kicks and his stretching. He foot-sparred with Daniel when they got together and had a free moment. Daniel was too slow in the legs to kick back effectively, but he could flick out a hand and touch Tom on the face, reminding him to block. And when Tom got a little too proud of himself, Dan'l would catch a kicking foot and lift, dumping Tom flat on his back. Even heavily padded as they both were, it was no great pleasure to get tossed on his back. It was just a matter of practice, learning how to fire his kicks quick and snatch the foot back without getting snared and uplifted. At the last fight with the merchant's son, Tom had been the one on his back; next time he wanted to return the favor.

And every night when it was too dark to work and they were inside the tilt, Tom read the Abe Lincoln book by the light of the fire. He read it out loud at first, and the men were quite willing to listen; but that took too long, fumbling over each word, so mostly Tom read silently, moving his lips as he read and afterward telling what he'd found.

For several days Daniel trapped with no success. Every day the woodsdevil ruined the catch, eating what he wished, destroying or fouling the rest.

Dan'l hid traps behind traps—four, five, and six in one place—but every day he found them empty, or sprung. Some he did not find at all.

The man who loved to smile frowned now as he tried every type of trap he could think of.

The day before the pile of cleaned wood was large enough to take, Daniel Squires tried his last trick.

He took twelve traps and rubbed them all over with rabbit meat to disguise the iron smell. Then he buried them beneath the snow, close to a bent-over tree with a twine noose hanging down that was meant to be found. He took the last of their rabbit and baited that trap's simple trigger, brushing over his tracks with a branch.

Then he walked back to camp to give the system time to work.

The pile of logs was four feet tall and twenty long. Part of it would ride on the sled; the rest would drag.

"You and Dan'l take 'er home," said Theo. "I'll bide here, keep the work movin' long as the weather holds. Mind, now, don't be visitin' pretty girls, Tom, nor yet goin' troutin'. No time fer that. Just drop the wood and come back. Ever'thin' depends on how much wood we gits. We needs piles and piles, more'n we ever got in our lives. Can't waste a day nor an hour if we is to make it through."

Tom did not argue. He was going home! He had never been away so long. All the good things called to him: food cooked by someone who really knew how to do it, a warm soft bed, and—Rosie. . . . He felt he could jump over trees.

The slide had to be packed carefully, the wood loaded in a certain way. Two logs had to stick out in front. They were the steerers. Tom would hold on to them and help guide the load. In the middle, the pile was roped together firmly, and a short stick, called the twister, was tucked under the rope. Each turn of the twister snugged up the rope. When the logs were tight together, the twister was secured. At the back of the pile two short logs were carried on top. These were tied together by one end of a rope, the other end fastened to the back of the slide. The short logs were for dragging, tossed back when downhill slopes let the slide build up too much speed. A load of wood rolling over could kill the dogs or men.

"Oo-eesht!" said Tom, holding the steerer in front of the slide. Daniel was just ahead with a rope across his shoulder, the other end fast to the sled. He would help pull as need arose.

The way home was easier than Tom had expected. The crust over the snow had thickened stiff and smooth; the slide moved easily.

Pale sun shone, warming patches between the blue-shadowed trees.

Tom felt excitement building in him, stirring him in new, strange ways. Things were, well, happening to him these last few months, things he could not talk about. For instance, sometimes his voice cracked if he talked at all! Some of the differences he liked—the new lines of muscle thickening arms and shoulders—but some were incredibly embarrassing, like the hair that was growing in undignified places.

And somehow all the changes seemed dimly to add up and make sense only when he thought about—Rosie.

Scary, almost, the feelings were so intense. He wanted to see her so much. He remembered her clearly—her dark brown eyes, the eyebrows she could arch so high, the way she laughed, how fast she could talk sometimes, and the way the front of her, the up-top part, was pushing out, womanlike. Rosie, Rosie.

It was dark when they got home.

Tom and Daniel went to unload the wood, to carry and stack it, but by then Ma was out there, and she said, "Just undo the strap and let 'em go. Lynny and me'll drag 'em around in the mornin'."

Tom suddenly realized how tired he was. They dumped the wood and untied Murphy.

"Ma, could ya get somethin' fer me animal?" asked Tom.

"After I gets ye fed, I'll thaw out them froze dogfish," Ma said.

"Weather looks threat'nin'," Daniel said, frowning at the sky. "I'll be by early." He waved good-bye, and the evening swallowed him.

Inside, Ma hotted up some baked cod for Tom. He lit the hall lamp and sneaked a peek at the children asleep— was it his imagination that Baby Sally seemed to have new hollows under her eyes? Mark Josephus still looked pretty big and well-fed.

Lynny woke and came out to the kitchen. She seemed her usual self, though mostly all she did was yawn after surprisingly hugging her brother. She hit him on the shoulder afterward, of course.

The juicy baked cod smelled so fine.

"Eat all you want; they is plenty," Ma said.

Tom remembered the covered quintal and a half of dried fish, the supposed cullage unsold from the summer. The flat dried fish must now feed the family. It was just about all they had, and they would eat the dried salt cod every meal, every day, and no complaints about it—the other choice being starvation.

Tom finished his food and made it up the steps, almost asleep before he pulled off his clothes.

It was not yet light when Tom heard his mother's voice. He thought she had come to say good-night, and he groaned when she said, "Time to be movin', son. You got to go now or be snowed in."

"What's fer breakfast?" he said, to put off getting up.

"Just twice-laid," said Ma. "Leftovers from supper. But I'll hot it up."

Being snowed in did not sound so bad to Tom. A few days of rest?

He ate the fragments of warm baked cod, then went into Lynny's room just for devilment and shook her shoulder to share the joy of being awake. She grumbled a promise of violence and rolled over. Then Tom looked in on Baby Sally. He stood there for a little bit, trying to hear if she was breathing. It was dark, and he could not see the covers rise. He leaned down close, putting his cheek beside her, and felt the warmth from her small face. Then he kissed her hair softly. As for Mark Josephus, Tom had already knuckled him on the top of his head, and his brother grunted something unintelligible and burrowed deep under the covers.

Tom hugged his mother hard while Daniel Squires looked away.

Going outside was like falling through the ice. The dogs were already hitched up. Tom was glad. He wanted to get moving now.

The snow came in biting gusts, ice crystals whipping their faces. Tom looked briefly back toward the sea, saw that the cove was filling up with pack ice blown in early from the bay. The wind rushed under the sides of his hood; snow scratched his face. He turned away from home.

A steady push of wind flattened his clothes against his back. He adjusted his balance. A sudden sharp blast almost picked him up. He wondered if he jumped, would the wind carry him? He started to go up on his toes to find out, then changed his mind. Part of the trail around Grayman's Beard Hill was called Place Where the Man Fell Over.

"Don't fergit, now," shouted Daniel through the dark and the snow and the wind, "this ain't winter!"

"Is you stunned in the head?" yelled Tom.

"This ain't winter," said Daniel loud and clearly as he could, "'cause we didn't have no summer, remember? Merchant boy cut off our credit. We got nothin' from the work, 'tis like summer never happened. So if that was'n' summer, this can't be winter. Must still be spring!"

"Funny kind o' spring!" yelled Tom.

They went on.

CHAPTER EIGHT

WOODSDEVIL SPRING

◆   ◆   ◆

As they approached the tilt, a thin column of smoke rose from the snow-covered cabin.

"'E's boilin' up, stoppin' fer tea," Tom said.

"I s'pose," said Daniel. "Hello, the house!" he called.

They heard no answer.

Inside they found Theo lying on the spruce bough bed, his extra shirt over his eyes. Napping when there was work to be done!

"Skipper! What's to do? Bein' lazy?" said Tom.

"Hey, b'y," said the voice, real soft and careful. "Dan'l with you?"

"Standin' right 'longside o' me. Take off yer nappin' cloth and look for yerself," said Tom.

"Can't see nothin'," said Theo. "Gun blowed up on me."

Dan'l looked beneath the homemade bandages. He sucked in his breath between clenched teeth. "Lard Jasus, protect us," he said.

They resoaked the shirt in warm tea and placed it back on the blasted face. Tom tried not to look at his father's eyes.

"I seen yer woodsdevil down t' the river. Just as bold 'e was, lookin' at me like no reason fer me to be there. I had me weapon along—loaded just in case—an' I moved real slow pickin' 'er up. But when I squeezed the trigger, barrel blowed up. Ye remember we only had the three shots of powder left, no credit to buy more. I couldn't afford to waste powder on no clean-out shot. Wish I had now, though. Guess there was some burnt powder blockin' 'er, an' she blowed up.

"I fumbled me way back here. Couldn't see. Found a coal in the ashes an' roused the fire. Then I made me some tea an' soaked me extry shirt. Been waitin' fer ye ever since."

"Grandfather always said tea was good fer burns," Tom said.

Then he remembered. "The hospital in St. John's!" said Tom. "Peggeen told me 'bout it. They got this place, see, where they makes sick folks better! All fellers in white clothes. An' they gives you food!"

"Ya got to pay fer that, son," said Dan'l. "Them 'ospitals is fer the merchants an' them that is barn rich. Can clean you out even though you got money. Which we ain't."

"Fer rich folks," said Theo.

"Don't seem right," said Tom. "Seems like all ya should have to be is sick an' they takes care of ya."

"'Member when ya got yer tooth hauled?" said Dan'l. "That's the kind o' doctorin' we can afford."

Tom remembered. The toothache had been terrible.

Noddy Weathers and Theo had taken turns with the borrowed pliers, trying to pull the tooth. It broke, only half coming out. The pressure and pain of the toothache eased, but the jagged fragment kept cutting Tom's tongue and making it bleed, so they had to do it again.

Tom shook his head, remembering.

"Well, how about the blood witch lives over to St. Phillips? Maybe she can help, put spiderwebs on yer eyes or somethin'. They sez she can witch cuts closed—"

"Ne' mind, b'y, ne' mind," said Theo. "I'll just bide here a couple days, play like I'm a merchant. Ye do the work; I'll do the sleepin'."

But three days passed, and though the swelling came down and the wounds on his face healed over, Theo still walked into a stunted spruce tree when he came outside and tried to work.

So Tom and Daniel loaded him on the slide.

Theo was furious. "Ye can only take half a load o' wood this way!" he said. But when he tried to walk, it took too long. In the end he glumly rode home.

"I knowed somethin' was wrong," said Ma when they arrived.

"Get me some net; I can be mendin," said Theo, and they brought a half-leaf of cod trap to him, laying it across his bed. Tom knew things were serious because they did not use the daybed in the kitchen.

The scarred hands knew their work. Tom filled an eight-inch double needle with twine and watched his father. His own eyes misted over, and he spoke quickly. "Uh, Skipper?"

"Yis, b'y?"

"How much wood'll ya be wantin' now?"

"Every scrap o' timber ye can bring. I can't see, but I

ain't dead. We keeps on wi' the plan. I'll work wi' the net, that's somethin' needs doin'. That'll take me a month or so—the whole middle section's tore up—and by that time I'll be seein' again. I found some powder grains on me cheek this mornin', mixed in wi' the wet comin' out o' me eyes. They'm gettin' better. An' even if they don't, I can cooper wi' me eyes shut. I got plenty pictures in me mind what barrels looks like."

Daniel reached into his backpack, into the privacy compartment that no one else would touch. He came out with a small glass bottle carefully wrapped in his extra socks. He looked at Marian Piccot, who frowned at first, then nodded.

"I been savin' some screech," Daniel said, and he put the bottle in Theo's hands.

"Oh, now . . . , " said Theo, grinning. "Marian, ya don't mind?"

"Go ahead, ya great ox. I'll get a glass fer them who's half-civilized." Theo hefted the half-filled bottle, measuring the contents by weight, figuring his share. He took a swig of the fiery stuff, one-eighth exactly of the contents remaining. He coughed, shook his head, then handed the bottle to Daniel, who, strangely, did not drink. Instead, he poured the exact same amount Theo had taken into the glass Ma gave him. Ma looked at him. Daniel put his fingers to his lips.

"Whoo! That's some better," said Daniel Squires, pretending, and gave the bottle back to his friend, who put down his net work.

Theo leaned back against the bed's headboard. The lamplight played on his features. Ma put her hand across her own mouth. She shook for a moment in silence; Tom put his hand on her shoulder. She drew a deep breath and calmed herself. Daniel talked just a bit louder.

Wind rattled. It was cold in the room.

They talked and laughed for a while, and the contents of the bottle of screech, fiery rum of excessively low cost and quality, transferred to the stomach of Theo and Daniel Squires's tall glass. Tom's mother went downstairs to do some work.

Tom did not see his father drink very often and was surprised how the alcohol loosened Theo's tongue. Normally Dan'l was the talkative one.

"Tom, is ya there, b'y?"

"Yis, Skipper, right here."

"I wish ya could've knowed me brother, John," he said.

Tom's head jerked up. His father never talked about this.

"Poor brother John, Skipper?" Tom asked respectfully, as one should speak of beloved dead.

Theo nodded.

"Ahrr. Like you he was, dreamin', always dreamin'. But a good worker just the same."

A gust of wind whistled outside.

"Where do—where did 'e live?" asked Tom.

"Right here. At t' cove," said Theo.

"He died fourteen year ago on Old Christmas Night, January six. The night that the Lard Jasus was truly born, not December twenty-fif like all them mainlanders think.

"Me brother, John, he was comin' home from the ice, back from the seal hunt. He was doin' real good, had his own ship. I hadn' gone along, fer ya know yer grandfather was set ag'in' goin' to the ice. He always took us to the graveyard, showed us that captain that died with his fingers gone.

"Sealers loses they fingers a lot. See, what happens is, ya carries the pelt by yer fingers through the eye holes. They is kind of sharp where the eyeballs used to be, an' they grates 'gainst the finger. Sometimes the finger gets infected, swells up hard like a rock, an' dies. No good. Ya know how ya fixes a infected 'seal finger'? Chop it off.

"Anyway, me brother, John, 'e went 'is own way, dreamin', dreamin'. Said if one Piccot could be rich, why not another. 'E were going to catch thousands o' seals. Oh, 'e was goin' to be rich—rich as the old Skipper was. Elias Piccot. Oh, 'e was rich, fer a while 'e was, had eighteen hunnert pounds, real money."

"What happened to the money?" asked Tom. Grandfather had never talked about the money or the ship except that one time he'd whipped Tom.

"His wife took sick. So 'e brung 'er to the 'ospital you was talkin' 'bout, the one in St. John's? She was in the 'ospital a year or more—don't be hoggin' that bottle, Dan'l Squires—cost me dad ever' cent 'e had, an' t' woman still died. Still . . . died. The ondly money Skipper Elias had left was in 'is schooner, the *Mollie B.*, named after 'is missuz, she who died."

He lifted the bottle again, shook it, frowned at it for being empty, set it down. He started to drift off.

"What happened to John?"

"I'm gettin' to 'er."

"Sorry."

"It was Christmas Day, an' he comin' home with a bumper load o' seals like nobody ever got. 'E'd struck a fine patch o' fat—seal blubber, I mean—we could tell afterward 'cause a lot o' the pelts washed up on t'shore."

Dead silence, but for the wind.

"Starm come. Big . . . starm. 'E should o' wore out to sea, stay there two, three days till she passed by. But 'e was always proud of 'is skill, an' 'e tried to bring 'er in. Ship struck a sunker—big sharp rock just under the surface. This was over by the motion, you mind the one where the two currents meet, just off Piccot's Gulch? The sunker tore the bottom right out of 'is ship. In Piccot's Gulch. That's why they named un that. Piccot's Gulch, I mean.

"Not more'n a hundred yards off. We watched. Nothin' we could do 'cept watch 'em go down. One by one. Most drowned; one or two made it. Noddy Weathers, 'e made it. I rigged a rope on me dory, gived the other end to your ma an' rowed out. But the swells was breakin' an' me dory capsized. I clung to the side whilst your ma pulled me back.

"Me poor brother, John. Last I saw of un, 'e was standing there, grippin' the mainmast. A swell swep' over, 'e's gone. Still under there some'eres, I s'pose, or in a shark's belly. I don't know."

Or p'rhaps the kraken got him, thought Tom, remembering the tentacles reaching up.

Theo paused, head bobbing. The dark beard pressed against his chest. He twitched once through the shoulders.

"After a time the sea got tired of messin' 'bout wi'the schooner and cast 'er up, like a play toy. Took the shore at Piccot's Gulch. Tha's how he got the name, account of John Piccot died there."

His breathing slowed. His eyes opened once, twice, then slipped shut. His right hand fumbled for the net, couldn't find the torn section; fumbled for the needle, couldn't. His lips moved as if he was about to say something, but no words came. The bottle tilted from his left hand.

Dan'l took the empty bottle, poured his share of the rum back into it, re-corked it, and took it downstairs.

"'E might need this later," he said, "when the pain gets too bad."

Ma put the bottle in the cupboard.

"'Twas heavy weather that night, b'ys" —they heard Theo say from upstairs.

Tom and Daniel were glad to get back to the woods.

Toward the end of December it snowed three days straight. Tom had not thought there was that much snow in the world. It wasn't particularly cold, but each separate snow crystal seemed to have its own stickum, clinging to the flakes before, adhering to the face and beard of Dan'l and Tom's thinly sprouting new jaw-fuzz.

When he had to go outside to void his nuisance, Tom tied a rope around his waist and tied the other end around Daniel Squires's foot. That way, if Tom took a couple steps in the wrong direction, he would not die lost in the snow. He could not see more than a foot or two.

There was no more tobacco. This did not bother Tom, who did not smoke, but it did bother Dan'l. Having to go through the pain of withdrawal from the vegetable drug did not improve his temper. But the tobacco was no more, and the snow prevented them from hunting for Indian leaf, so even that substitute was denied him. The chaw, or plug tobacco, was already gone.

"Uncle?"

"Ahrr?"

"We be home fer mummerin'?"

Daniel shook his head. "No Christmas off this year."

Christmas in the outports lasted twelve days, with something going on every night: costumed mummers going door to door; special cakes; a dance with a "fiddler" who played an accordion; people playing spin the bottle, tucker, you-you-you, who's got the button? and other innocent mischiefs. Food was made beforehand, so for those twelve days as little work as possible was done.

But for Tom there would be no vacation this winter.

The wolverine left their trapline alone—but not through kindness.

Daniel had got inspired and tried to catch it one more time. If a dozen traps would not work, he would try two dozen—all they had left. But first he made a cubby, an open-roofed little cabin, two feet wide and three feet long. Inside he put the bait, an entire rabbit carcass, and no trap. The traps were scattered all around, rubbed with rabbit meat.

Most of the traps the wolverine found, springing them with chunks of ice or a tree branch apparently held in its teeth.

But one of the traps worked.

When Daniel came back from checking the traps, he tossed Tom a dark hairy toe and a claw.

Tom carried the wolverine claw in his pocket, for luck.

And it did seem that their luck had finally turned better. The furs piled up, and at night when they were done scraping fat off the pelts, Tom read aloud from the book.

Slowly, halting and stumbling, he stammered through page after page.

"This Lincoln, 'e were like one of we," he said. "Lived in a tilt. Plain folk. Hardly no speechifyin' 'cept when 'e got into politics, when ya got to talk a lot, I s'pose. 'E were mischeevous, too. Looky here how 'e took 'is little brother, walked 'im upside down across the ceilin', just fer to be foolin' 'is ma! And how 'e brung the widder three cents back 'stead o' cheatin' 'er."

"Well, o' course, big chunk o' money like that, natural he'd bring 'er," said Dan'l.

"Well, but I'm sayin', 'e was a merchant, but 'e wasn' mean."

"I've heard they is some good merchants that don't cheat their people. I just never met one, that's all." Dan'l stretched and sighed.

"Maybe merchants is different down thar in the States?" asked Tom.

"Well, there's more of 'em, so they kind of fights among theirselves. Competition, they calls it. So if one is mean, won't pay ya square or charges too much, ya just goes to another. Keeps 'em honest, I s'pose."

"Wish we had somethin' like that here," said Tom.

"If wishes was fishes, ever'body'd have riches," said Daniel Squires.

Just when it seemed they could not stand another fall of snow, the grip of winter loosened. Snowflowers burst to the light, spreading crimson petals as if in defiance of the cold.

The winter had been so fierce even Manuel's River had frozen over. Now the ice cracked with a noise like rifle shots and started to move. They heard the whir of ptarmigan, which had just begun to change color from winter white to spotted brown. Mud showed through snow in wider patches. The sun hinted at warmth.

Tom and Daniel worked even faster, trying to get as many loads home as they could before the melting snow and mud made travel impractical. You could only drag one or two logs at a time without the snow to slide on.

And then one day, when the sky turned an infinite blue, they heard thunder where there was no storm.

"Oh, if I only had a gun that would work!" said Daniel.

"What is it, what is it?" asked Tom.

"The deer is comin'. The caribou."

The rumbling increased, growing ever louder, and the noise had a strange undertone—a clicking sound. "That's their knee joints, knockin' as they run. You'll see 'em soon. But don't get close. The bulls is in the spring matin' mood, about to get the moss off they horns, wantin' to fight. Nothin' like how shy they is the rest o' the year."

"Whoa! Look, look!" shouted Tom.

Over a low rise they came, like a wave, and the world was filled with brown, sturdy, antler-bearing life. And more. For there were other watchers present.

A black bear stood up from a just-exposed patch of red berries.

"Where did 'e come from?" said Tom. "Do bears taste good? Could we kill un?"

"Shh!" said Daniel.

The black bear approached the caribou as they pawed snow, nibbling pale green lichen beneath.

An enormous bull caribou trotted away from the herd. Snorting, it approached the bear. The caribou seemed trembling with energy, as if charged up with fury over some insult. With its left front hoof it kicked snow behind it.

"Hoo-eee," whispered Tom. "They'm gonna fight!"

"In spring a buck deer'll fight anythin'. It's their love life, I think, gets 'em riled up," said Dan'l back, quiet as he could.

The caribou charged. The bear turned and ran.

The buck pushed on, caught up. Antlers still mossy green poked hard at the bear's running haunches.

The bear tripped and fell hard, then rolled and turned. Suddenly it was standing up straight on its hind legs almost right beside the deer.

The caribou swerved, was several yards away, then stopped and stood stiffly. The bear made a low moaning noise and crouched, wide-legged, arms wide.

The caribou lowered his antlers and rushed.

Crouched like a wrestler, the bear braced and took the impact, black-furred arms wrapping the antlers. Then, with a heave of giant strength, the bear twisted its bulk to one side and down. There was a crack, and the deer went down, neck broken, eyes already glazing as it fell.

The contest was over. The bear began to feed.

Then Daniel sharply tapped Tom's shoulder. Tom turned his head.

Out of the shadow of the woods, so full of energy it fairly bounced over the snow, came the devil of the woods. Its fur was a beautiful reddish brown tipped with black. Its body was squat and thick and low. The narrow head moved back and forth. The wolverine came as if it knew nothing of fear.

But it was small! Did it not see the bear? Tom wondered.

The black bear paid it no attention until the comparatively tiny creature stopped just six feet away—and snarled.

Tom's mouth dropped open. This little animal was threatening a bear?

The bear looked up with small red eyes. A warning cough rumbled.

The wolverine hissed, nostrils and lips peeling back from white teeth. Slower now, eyes fixed on the bear, the wolverine stepped closer. It sank white teeth into one haunch of the caribou carcass and dragged the body backward an inch. Then it released the meat and clicked strong jaws together—*snap!* The message was unmistakable. It would have the food, or there would be trouble.

The bear paused, mouth open, head slightly turned to one side.

The wolverine leaped, front feet on the caribou's carcass. White teeth clashed an inch from the bear's nose.

The bear's right paw, big as a shovel, slammed down on the wolverine—or rather where the wolverine had been. The king of the weasels moved in a red-brown flash, evading death, but making no attempt to get away.

Prowling now on the right, now leaping left, darting in and gone in an instant, the wolverine settled in to make the bear's life miserable. Taking incredible risks, he came right in next to his opponent. *Snap!* He nipped a chunk from the black bear's lip. The woodsdevil retreated just enough, then harassed the eight-hundred-pound animal as it tried to go back to its meal.

Tom noticed the wolverine never stood still, never matched strength with the heavier beast. The woodsdevil fought the way *it* wanted to fight, slashing and using its powers of speed, making its own decisions.

Suddenly the bear seemed alone. Unable to see its forty-pound tormentor, the bruin hugged the caribou closer and tried to see in all directions.

The wolverine came up from behind and bit the bear right on the butt.

The earth seemed to shake as the bear roared and chased, and chased—

And chased . . .

A bear is not built for long-distance pursuit. Panting, it stopped and turned around. There was the woodsdevil back at the deer, eating calmly, as if the bear had never been.

The bear roared, of course, but there was a different note in his growls now. He did not rush back this time. Something seemed to have changed between them. The wolverine hissed but made no attack, merely hopping back a couple of feet.

The bear sank its teeth in the caribou's leg, shook its

dark head, and tore off the haunch.

Still muttering, the black bear took to the woods. The wolverine paused to watch it depart, then turned and went back to the deer.

"Country meat," said Daniel.

To Tom's astonishment and delight, Daniel stood up from where they had crouched and walked quickly toward the dead caribou and the wolverine.

"Remember us?" he said to the infuriated woodsdevil. "You visited our tilt t' other day. Now we'll be returnin' yer visit." He shifted the ax in his hand.

The wolverine studied the advancing humans, snarled at their scent, and put its paws on the carcass it had just won.

"Ya lost a toe last time ya fooled with us. Want to lose some more?" asked Daniel.

"Shoo! Go on!" said Tom. For a reason he could not have explained, he did not want to see the woodsdevil die. It made no sense. He should have hated it, he thought.

The wolverine growled till it seemed about to strangle. Then it darted its head into the caribou's belly.

The last Tom saw of the devil of the woods, it was dragging the heart and some intestines off into the bush.

"Twice-took meat's the sweetest," said Dan'l. "He took it from the bear; we've took it from him."

"There's enough here fer all the cove!" said Tom. It was the custom to share country meat if someone got lucky and killed a deer.

"Well, I just wonder who's goin' to get the first visit," said Daniel as they dressed out the meat.

"Well, me mother, o' course," said Tom. Oh, no, he thought, here it comes.

"And natural, we don't want to forget that nice Widder Crandall," said Daniel, "her and 'er sweet little daughter—

what's 'er name? Somethin' like a flower, as I recollect."

"You squawks like a old sea gull," said Tom.

CHAPTER NINE

CAN'T WHISTLE DOWN THE NORTHERN LIGHTS

◆   ◆   ◆

"I got to take me a bath!" said Tom, once the first hellos were said. Daniel Squires had gone home, and "the littles," Sally and Mark Josephus, had climbed all over their big brother until he finally gave in and held them both at once. Theo, sitting on the kitchen's daybed, grunted something Tom couldn't understand. Ma looked at Tom. Tom pointed to his own eyes, then quickly at Theo. Ma shook her head.

"You do need a bath, fer certain!" said Lynny. "Come on to the river; we'll bring some water," she said.

"You mean I'll bring the water while you fills me ears wi' gossip," said Tom, who understood the ways of big sisters.

Putting the yoke across his shoulders, Tom stooped for the buckets and Lynny got the door. She had to lift it slightly because the strap hinge was loose, and the weight of the door made it stick.

When they were outside and the door was shut behind them, Tom said, "I'm surprised Skipper haven't got that door planed down. 'E's been home near two months now."

"'E ain't the same," said Lynny. "'E don't take thought fer nothin' but the nets and the wood. Hardly never sleeps. And grouchy? Whew! Like a bear wi' the toothache, never a good word fer nobody."

"How good can 'e see?"

"Well, I heard 'im tell Ma that 'e had one eye squinted when the rifle blowed up, an' that eye is some better. 'E can see shapes now, blurry. But t' other one, just light an' dark, that's all."

Tom stooped beside the crystal stream winding over mossy rocks. The sea was just a hundred yards away. He heard the crash of low surf without really being aware of it, just a sweet, familiar part of being home. The gulls cried overhead, checking out Tom as he broke the film of ice on the stream and filled a bucket. His eyes took in the green hills, the grey rock breaking through, and patches of snow everywhere. He smiled at the chill blue cove with its boats and spider-legged stages.

Tom broke the ice again and filled the other bucket.

"Soon as I get cleaned up, I'm goin' to take Missuz Crandall some meat," he said.

Lynny frowned, her narrow face seeming to become thinner still. "That's good," she said, "but—but you know Rosie ain't there."

Tom was crouching, hooking the notches of the yoke under the bucket handles. He stopped. "What?"

"She's still in St. John's."

"St. John's? Why fer'd she go there?"

"Edmund took 'er to be 'is maid."

Tom thought about this for a moment. "I'm goin'," he said.

With his backpack full of food: a frozen, cloth-wrapped haunch of deer meat, his mother's last jar of bake-apple jam, and a couple thawed dogfish for Murphy, Tom set out next morning for the city of St. John's.

Lynny and Ma had tried to talk him out of it, but Theo just said, "Can't whistle down the Northern Lights. Might as well learn fer hisself."

In Tom's left hand was a big square of lassy bread, strong and sweet and good. Murphy walked on his right.

Tom had been to St. John's before and knew the way.

Even with the urgency of his mission Tom was happy, and so was Murphy, ambling calmly by his side. Flowers burst up everywhere: red maltese crosses vied with dandelions and delicately hued wild orchids. Motion caught Tom's attention. A black-and-yellow tiger swallowtail butterfly flitted across the path. Blue jays shrieked raucously.

"This is the prettiest place in the world, me son," murmured Tom to his dog. "If only a man could earn a living here." And that, down deep, was the question. If he and his family could survive, everything else would follow.

Just before noon he came to the treeless ridge. He slowed down as he got to the top.

Below him stretched St. John's. To the left and down he saw the blue of Lake Quidi Vidi; beyond it was The Narrows, walls of rock around the harbor. On one side was The Battery and Signal Hill: flags, Fort Amherst, and mounted cannon. There the explorer John Cabot had stood when he had claimed Newfoundland for England in fourteen hundred something or other. Tom had been told in school, but forgot.

And spread out like models below were buildings. There must have been . . . a hundred! Maybe more!

There were two main streets: Duckworth Street, named for a governor who died; and Water Street, which fronted on the harbor with Lake Quidi Vidi on its hind side. The buildings were bigger than whales, and some of them made of white marble quarried from Rose Blanche up the coast.

The merchant's house was on the side of Signal Hill. Huge and white it was, part marble and part wood, and it had real paint. It was not even a place of business. Most merchants lived in the upper stories of their business residence, but not this one.

Tom stood by the door to the great house and was afraid. He became suddenly conscious that his clothes were many-times patched, and his right sealskin boot had a hole in the top where his toe had worn through. Twice he steeled up his nerve to knock on the great door, and twice his hand fell limply back to his side.

Murphy looked up at him quizzically.

"I'm doin' it," said Tom, and rapped the door hard, making it sound to the echo.

For a moment there was silence.

Then Tom's heart leaped. He heard footsteps, and he knew who walked like that, seeming always on the edge of skipping.

The door flung open.

Rosie.

Her eyes were even larger than he remembered, shaped like deep brown almonds, dark and rich, but alive with light and laughter.

"Tom!" she said, and her smile made him shake.

She wore a black dress down to her ankles and a white

apron over that. But her beautiful long brown hair was tied up in a white lace maid's cap.

"Rosie," he said.

Then a deep voice spoke from down the polished hardwood hall. A voice that made Tom's stomach quiver and his face turn red in frustration, rage, and fear.

"Who is it, my girl?" said Edmund, the merchant's son.

"Just a friend from the outports, sir, fer me," she said, not taking her eyes off Tom.

Tom talked low and fast. "Rosie, come away wi' me, right now, come back home. You got no business workin' fer him."

She frowned. "I'm here of my own will. I got to work, don't I? Think the Piccots is the only family has debts? I works fer him a year; he promised my ma won't lose her credit. Plus I get cloth to make a new dress once a year, fer wages."

"I don't want you here. He—"

"Well, I wondered who our *friend* from the outports was." Edmund wore a velvet smoking jacket over a ruffled white shirt.

"If ya has a friend, which I misdoubt, tisn' me!" said Tom.

Edmund took a half step forward, stopped.

Murphy had also taken a half step forward. His redbrown eyes were locked on Edmund.

"Do you never go anywhere without that walking flea collection?" asked Edmund.

"'E's company," said Tom, "and how be them pertty black gloves?" Tom remembered the bone-jarring slam of the knuckle-dusters and was glad Murphy stood beside him.

"I'll show them to you again one day." Edmund smiled. "And now if I may inquire as to the nature of your business?"

"I come to visit Rosie."

"What a pity. She's not receiving visitors today."

"I brung her somethin'."

"Oh, a present? How nice. Do drop it off at the servant's entrance. It's around back. Anything else? No? Well, in that case I will bid you good afternoon. But of course I will see you again, *at settling-up time.*"

Now the mask of false courtesy dropped, and the fire underneath showed through.

"I hope you'll have the money you owe us so I won't have to take your property. It is such a nuisance selling off people's houses, and furniture—and dogs," he added, gazing at Murphy.

His eyes moved lazily back to Tom's face.

"Rosie, say good-bye to the . . . gentleman."

Tom looked at her. There was a wildness in him, a desperate longing to say or do something important. But there was nothing to do, nothing to say. Just . . . good-bye. He said it the old-fashioned way.

"God be wi' ya, Rosie," he said. "I'll see ye at settlin'-up, too—unless your master's afeared to let ya outta the house."

"I wouldn't have her miss it for all the world," said Edmund.

Then Rosie said something very peculiar. "Save yer wood, Tom."

Edmund looked at her strangely. So did Tom. Neither had any idea what she meant. They both pretended they did, of course.

Softly the door shut, and the last thing he saw was a glimpse of her face.

Tom trudged around back to the servant's entrance, where he dropped off the deer meat and the clay jar sealed with wax. His ma made wonderful bake-apple jam, the tangy orange berries sour and sweet at the same time, seeming to contain the spring. And the deer meat was the best cut of the whole animal and would cook up rich and savory. The second maid took them as if they were dirty, and Tom felt almost ashamed of the wonderful gifts.

He wondered if, well, maybe Rosie was better off in a rich place like this.

On the way home, Tom thought about Edmund and practiced his kicks in the air. A kick with the right foot, then spin around and kick with the other. A high kick and a low one after—Daniel said he was not supposed to hurt a person seriously, not do damage, because that was wrong. But wasn't fighting itself wrong? And what was you supposed to do if somebody was fighting you? Say thank you very much?

And what did that mean, what Rosie had said? Save your wood?

"Courtin' talk," said Ma, neatly biting a thread from the snow mitts she was sewing. Some neighbors down the road near Pt. St. Phillips had some goats but couldn't sew, and Marian sewed but had no goats anymore, having sold them for two barrels of flour. So the neighbors traded snow mitts and mufflers for goat milk and goat cheese; these both reserved for Baby Sally and Mark Josephus, both of whom had become too thin.

"Courtin' talk?" said Lynny with enormous interest. "Tom's got a girlfriend!"

"Tom 'n' Rosie's courtin', Tom 'n' Rosie's courtin'!" sing-songed Baby Sally.

"We ain't neither!" said Tom, wishing he hadn't brought up the subject. If he had known it was mushy stuff, he would have asked somebody else, like maybe Peggeen, the schoolteacher.

It was Sunday, the day of rest. Church was over, and Tom had been glad to change out of his good clothes, to chuck that stiff collar and the old leather shoes of his father's that looked nice but did not fit. His toes were all crunched under, and walking in them was no delight. It was a pleasure to slip on his sealskin moccasins again.

Right now he was trying to teach Mark Josephus how to make a reindeer pattern cat's cradle with string wrapped around his fingers. Baby Sally could do it easily, but Mark's hands were not as clever as hers. He had to develop skill with string to help him make and repair nets. Play in the outports came down to work, one way or another.

"Here, Mark, you try 'er."

Mark Josephus put his hands into the weave of string and tried to make the reindeer run. For a moment he held it, and then he sneezed. His hands twitched. The reindeer became a tangle of twine.

Lynny went upstairs to fetch something, and Tom saw his chance.

"Quick, Ma, afore she gets back! What exactly do it mean, save yer wood?"

"Well." She smiled at him. "When a girl likes a boy, she lets him know in little ways. Tellin' ya to save yer wood, well, that's pretty bold, but then Rosie May never was the bashful type."

"But—wood?"

"Well, before ya can settle down with a wife, ya has to build yer house to live in, don't ya? Only the last child to marry stays wi' the house, takin' care of we old folks. So ya starts early on to save the buildin' materials fer yer house. Ya saves up boards, sets 'em aside under shelter. In three, four years you've saved enough to make the floor and the walls, a kitchen—"

"And a bedroom!" said Lynny, who had not stayed upstairs long enough.

"Lynn Marie, such talk ain't proper," said Ma, but the look she gave her was one of shared understanding. "Anyway, then ya asks yer neighbors to help you put up the house, same as ya would for them. Just like ya helped that feller across t' cove move his house over the ice two winters ago, 'member that?"

"Oh, yeah, the house broke through the ice, halfway across. We had to saw her a channel to float over on, then drag 'er out. Took most ever' man in t' cove. She was good built though, sound as a boat, and wasn' hurt by the water."

"So after ya get the main rooms built, ya moves in; add t' other rooms as ya go."

"But wouldn't that take a very long time?" asked Mark Josephus, the string a messy tangle in his hands. It seemed he always talked like a short adult, not a child of six.

"Yis, b'y, an' that's good. See, if ya takes four, five years to build a house afore gettin' hitched, it means you'm serious about it, cuz you've had plenty time to change your mind. Tom's not yet thirteen year old, 'e's not ready for serious courtin'. But in four or five years, when 'e's got the wood all saved, well, that's somethin' different."

"So ya think that's what she really meaned?" asked Tom, all in a fret.

Theophilous had been lying on the daybed in the kitchen, eyes shut against the pain. The net was repaired, and he could find no more work to do. According to his beliefs, chopping wood was work and not to be done on Sunday; fixing the net was not work. But he had been in the house for two months and had no more linnet to weave into string, nor any more nets to mend. It was driving him crazy to do nothing.

"Don't get yer hopes up, b'y," Theo said. "That Edmund's up to somethin'. 'E don't need more maids. I hear they already has three maids in the one house, fallin' over theirselves tryin' to keep busy. Nope. Edmund— *Master* Edmund"—he opened the stove and spat inside— "he wants to marry Rosie his ownself."

Tom looked hard at his father.

Theo felt his glance. "I'm sorry to tell ye that, b'y, but it's the truth. Edmund's got money. 'E hired Rosie on by way o' showin' off, so's she'd see how easy life would be wi' him if they was hitched. You watch. In three, four years, whenever it suits him, he'll snap his fingers, an' she'll have no choice but to jump."

"Never! No such of a thing," said Tom. For an instant he felt like hitting his blind father and was instantly ashamed of such a thought. He also felt like bursting into tears, and that was most definitely not going to happen here.

"I'm goin' out wi' Murphy," he said, and left.

Mark Josephus jumped up to go along. Baby Sally stayed still where she was, having no energy to spare. Tom pushed Mark back.

"No," he said. "Not this time."

"Don't be goin' troutin'," said Mark Josephus, who was not without his pompous side. "That is a sin on the Sabbath, you know."

Up the path they went, Tom and his dog.

Presently they were over the ridge, out of sight of the outport village. Walking blindly, Tom felt hot tears flood down his cheeks. What was the matter with him? One minute he was so happy; the next he was crying like a baby.

Oh, why wasn't Grandfather around? He would have known what to do. Why did he have to be dead!

"Come on, Murphy. Let's leave the trail; go down to the river. I don't want to meet nobody wi' me acting like a fool," he said.

Murphy obligingly turned off the trail and down. They found concealment under some scrubby pines that were gnarled and too low to be worth logging.

Before them was a big flat rock jutting out into the stream. The water curled around it and had that smooth look of power, which meant deep.

Tom put his hand on Murphy's warm back. "Ya must think I'm a terrible baby, actin' like this," he said. Murphy panted happily. Whatever Tom was, was just fine with him.

Then the dog did something strange. He crawled out to the edge of the rock, looked down, and then lay flat on his belly. He dangled his paw in the water. His right paw, the one with a white mark on the back of it, he twitched in the water.

Tom watched quietly, enjoying the moment of peace. Then Murphy dived in.

Before the splash had subsided he was out, dripping wet—with a trout in his mouth.

"Whoa!" said Tom. "Where'd ya learn to do that?" Murphy deposited the arctic trout at Tom's feet and returned to his trolling. He dangled his paw, always the right one, baiting the trout, and when one came—*splash!* Murphy added another fish to the neat pile, making no attempt to eat them.

When Tom calmed down enough to go home, there was a neat line of ten arctic trout beside him. He found a stick and poked it through their gills for carrying.

"Oh, Tom went troutin'!" Mark Josephus purely loved to tattle, especially since he had not been allowed to go along.

"No such of a thing," said Tom.

"What ha' ya been doin'?" asked Theo, and Ma looked at him sharply. Religion among the outporters was no casual thing. Stories were told of those who had starved to death rather than work on the seventh day.

"Murphy done it," said Tom. "Was that a sin?"

"'Tis wicked!" said Mark Josephus righteously.

"No, I think 'tis a Sunday gift," said Ma, "from He who makes the waves and holds us in the palm of His hand."

"From Murphy, too," said Tom, wanting his dog to get some credit.

"I s'pose," said Ma.

And Theo said nothing at all. But his face relaxed.

If there was anything that smelled better than fresh trout frying, neither Tom nor Theo knew what it was.

"Tom, see can you get me some cods' heads and fish guts and some kelp. I needs to make pit manure for the garden," said Ma on Monday morning. "You and Lynny take the handbarrow, see what ye can find."

"Take Mark Josephus instead, afore or after school. I'm needin' Tom t' home," said Theo. "Got a piece o' pit sawin' to do, takes two men. There's childern chores and man chores. I'm needin' Tom to do a man's work now."

"Mark Josephus can't carry so much," said Ma.

"Then he'll take more trips. Every pound's a help," said Theo. "Tom an' I got plenty sawin' to do."

Tom puffed out his cheeks and blew softly. He had seen the pit.

In the community-owned store (nothing bought there, only a place for storage and work), there was a hole in the second-story floor and a set of mounted vise clamps beside it. A long saw with jagged teeth lay beside the clamps, and few men picked up that saw with joy.

"You'll have to be the one works on the first floor," said

Theo when Tom had led him up the stairs and over to the vise and saw.

"Yis, b'y," said Tom.

He went below and dragged in a ten-foot log from one of their piles outside. "Here it comes, Skipper," he said, poking it up through the hole in the floor. "Can ya see it?"

"I can feel it," said Theophilous. "Ya hit me in the shin-bone."

"Sorry, Skipper."

"Mind how we does this. We got to move together, else the blade'll buckle an' get stuck. We're sawin' longwise, and that's t' hardest way; also the *only* way if we wants planks fer the stage."

"Do we move the saw or the log?" asked Tom, shaking his head.

"We'll move the saw. You pulls on the downstroke an' I rests. You rests on the upstroke as I pulls. Got it?"

"Sure enough, Skipper."

"Let's go."

Each saw stroke sent a spray of sawdust in Tom's face. Tom could only squint his eyes and accept it.

They sawed all day.

The days passed and the rainy season came, wonderful gray floodings from the sky, but Tom barely knew it. He and Theo labored inside as many hours as they could force.

Six days a week they coopered, interrupted only by household chores that Ma and the littles could not handle.

And once Tom said, "I'm so tired—if the kraken come up to take me now, I'd not kick up a fuss, just so I could sleep on the way down." Even Theo snorted at that. But he never slowed the working.

They sawed and scraped and planed—cedar, spruce,

and pine—sometimes steamed and bent it, too, shaping it for different purposes. Barrel staves must be cut narrow, neatly rectangular. Longers were just stripped trees, strength and length to be support beams for a fishing stage. Strouters were like longers, only heavier—to take the force of storm waves crashing at the stage head. Fence posts were easy—sharp at one end and reasonably straight, ready to pound into the ground. Wood, wood, wood!

Tom worked to exhaustion every day and ate baked cod that was loaded with protein. Wiry muscles made themselves shown.

And every fifth board Theo set aside in a pile Tom wasn't supposed to notice. He smiled through the sawdust and sweat. His father talked some grouchier than he really was.

Daniel Squires's cheerful presence was missed. He had a way of making hard work easier with his little jokes and stories. But his part in the wood work was over for now, and he had his own labors at home.

Everyone did. When Lynny and Mark Josephus brought home the kelp, cod heads, and fishguts, they and Baby Sally took hoes and chopped up the fish and seaweed, mooshing it into the thin layer of soil that would become their garden. Vegetables were luxuries, and if you wanted a potato or a parsnip, you first had to make the dirt to grow it in. Sometimes you could go into St. John's and trade for some of the ballast dirt in the holds of the ships, but such riches were not often shared. In a country of rock, dirt is expensive! When Ma swept the house, she gathered the dust and took it outside for the garden.

For long, long weeks Tom coopered, satisfying his curiosity forever about the art of barrel making. When iron barrel straps proved too expensive, Daniel Squires's furs paid for linnet, which the men wove into twine. When the barrel boards were steamed and bound around the iron frame, Theo wrapped the woven string tightly around the barrels: middle, top, and bottom.

There was more barking to do, soaking all nets and linnet in the steaming pot of spruce ends and tar, getting ready for the fish. For no matter what else they must do to survive, Tom and Theo were fishermen still. They were waiting. Getting ready for the sea.

Every morning Tom and Theo drank their fisherman's cup of cod-liver oil, dipping into the rot pot where the fish livers were decomposing, drinking down heavy gulps of the foul-tasting liquid. They also rubbed their hands with it every day to keep the dry, rough fisherman skin from chapping and cracking too much.

Everyone grew thin. Nobody moved more than they had to, saving all energy for work because the food was too short for anything extra. Mark Josephus was round no more, and Baby Sally—you could almost see through her, she was so frail and light.

But April passed, and May, and nobody died.

Some mornings, when there was nothing to eat, there would be a thump on the porch. Whoever ran to the door would see nothing but the back of a retreating fisherman, hurrying away from the gift of food he'd left: salted cod, usually, or a couple of withered sweet carrots, root-cellared through the winter.

And then, one day in early June, a shout woke their slumbering minds.

"The capelin! They've come at last! Capelin, in t' cove!"

It was the start of everything.

CHAPTER TEN

THE SHARK AND OTHER VISITORS

◆　　◆　　◆

"Caaayyypelin!" A fisherman stood in his boat out at the mouth of Portugal Cove. He drew a deep breath, cupped his hands, and called with all the power of a voice accustomed to making itself heard over the noises of the sea. It rumbled from his stomach, expanded in his chest, exploded joyous past his vocal cords. *"Caayyypelin! Comin' t' the cove!"*

Like a trumpet blast the joyous news wound out, echoing, rebounding from the hills, carrying clearly to Tom and Theo Piccot cleaning wood in front of the house.

"CAPELIN'S T' THE COVE!" shouted Tom, dropping the hand plane as if it were hot.

"I isn' deef," said Theophilous, leaning another peeled tree against the pile. "Till now," he added, rubbing his ear.

"Capelin's t' the cove!" yelled Mark Josephus next, bursting out the door and down the path.

"Yis, b'y," sighed Theo, picking up Tom's hand plane, stowing it under a tarp. Even on the sunniest day in Newfoundland, it's never wise to bet against the rain.

"Capelin, caayyyypelin!" hollered Baby Sally with more energy than she had in months. She wasn't entirely certain what capelin were, but she wasn't about to miss out on the fun. She looked up at Theo, and her neck looked too frail for the weight of her head and her enormous excited eyes. Theo's big rough hand groped out, smoothed down her hair, softly, ever so gently.

"Then we'd best get the handbarrow," he said.

Ma came out with two wicker baskets, one under each arm.

"I know, I know," sighed Theo.

"Capelin's t' the cove," said Ma.

Everyone hurried to the shore. Even old George trundled along, though with more dignity, as befits a man of 104, but he, too, would get to the landwash eventually. No one would miss this moment.

And on the shore they waited.

The mood was a mix of desperation and joy, as if someone were going to pass out free money. Everyone needed and intended to get some, and hoped there would be enough.

Tom stood with the others on the rocks and the mud as the white foaming surf rushed and swirled by their boots. But the waves were empty still. Only bubbles and froth popped and hissed and flattened.

Gulls shrieked and swooped; they waited, too.

And then, high in the blue vault of sky, a solan goose looked down. Folded its six-foot wings. And fell.

One moment the bird was a great glider, soaring; the next, a hurtling missile. It dropped faster and faster—fifty, a hundred, two hundred miles an hour. But it was not falling out of control. Through the winds of its own passage it rocketed, adjusting feathers constantly, aiming toward its six-inch target, down and down, wings slightly out until the last instant, then folded in completely. The neck was pulled tight; the rock-hard, sharp beak cleaved.

White water fountained. The sound of the splash reached the people packed together on the shore.

A roaring cheer went up as the solan goose, or gannet, rose successful from its dive. A wonderful wriggling bulge went down the bird's long neck. The gannet was feeding! It was true, at last. Capelin!

Now suddenly the waves were filled with darting silver-and-seagreen shadows—small, narrow, two-toned fish, six to eight inches long. Shoals of them, millions!

Then one green-and-silver female swam in with a wave, right onto the shore. On the slab mud and wet rock the fish wriggled, releasing tiny sticky eggs. Quick as she moved, two males came up, one on each side of her head. As she laid her eggs, the males fertilized them, releasing a cloud of white milt. It was done, and they turned and tried to escape, wriggling for the water they had left.

But the predators had other plans. Gull wings flapped into a fluttering roar as the sea birds swooped and feasted. For an instant Tom wished they had set up a scare-gull, a spooky-looking wood and straw figure that frightened sea gulls away from the garden. But no scare-gull could chase so many birds away from so much food.

Just offshore, the low fin of a shark showed briefly at the surface. The fin moved jerkily but without rush, as its owner fed without the need to hunt, just moving its head and gulping, much as it wanted. Nor were the humans slow to follow, wading out into the fish.

Baby Sally caught a capelin in her hands. It slipped and dropped and got away. She ducked and grabbed, aiming for one, catching another. Mark Josephus calmly held a basket sideways to the waves, waiting for the capelin to swim in. They did. Lynny picked fish like blueberries, bending over and grabbing, filling the basket on her left arm.

Tom had a small throw net, lead weights on the underside giving it weight. There were strings connected to each weight, and all the twine came together through a ring (a hollowed-out piece of backbone from a goat) past which the separate strings connected into one. Holding on to that one string, Tom threw. The net encircled a patch of fish. The weights sank down around them. He pulled the string, the weights came together, and Tom had a bagful of fish.

Ma and Theo worked a hand-seine, a twenty-foot section of net. Theo walked his end waist-deep and circled back, not minding the wet. Then they both began to pull, but the net had too many fish, and they bulged over the top of the net and were too heavy. Daniel Squires came and helped Ma, and to everyone's delight, the dog Murphy bit one end of Theo's side of the net carefully in his teeth and backed up, hauling the fish ashore. For him it was enough to see, and then to imitate.

"I'll make some praties o' this run!" said Ma, who was fishing for her garden. "Praties," or potatoes, needed capelin to help the soil.

The Piccots' fish went into their handbarrow, a barrel with two boards attached for ease of carrying. Quick as they could fill it, Tom and Lynny rushed it home to dump it in a larger barrel in the shade of the root cellar. First-caught fish were always fattest; they were for home eating. Those fish caught last, at the end of the run, would be the skinniest, used for dogs and bait and fertilizer.

For two days the capelin came. Nothing else mattered. Sleep was no more than a few snatched hours, and silver-green fish wriggled through dreams.

At last the silver, shining run dwindled, thinned, and stopped. But the activity did not.

Quick as the men could snatch a bite to eat and get away, they all rushed down to their boats. The capelin had not come alone.

"See ya on t' squiddin' grounds!" yelled Jamie Anderson.

The squid . . . Tom saw horrible green eyes and long arms reaching up. For him. He shook away the memory.

Tom, Daniel, and Theo rowed out in the dory. They had five oars, and every one was in use.

Tom rowed the forward oars, Daniel the middle, Theo sculled and steered with the single oar stuck back through the notch in the stern. Theo's vision was bad, but he could tell the difference between boat and no boat in front of them, and he knew the waters in more ways than sight. Tom yelled out "Port!" or "Starboard!" left or right for directions, and Theo let him; but he could have found his way by memory, scent, and "sea sense" alone.

"Easy as she goes, Skipper!" Tom said, meaning stop, and he tossed the new kellick overboard. They had found what was left of Tom's old wood/stone anchor, but it had been mangled by the crushing press of ice, so Tom had made another. As it settled to the seafloor, securing the boat, he picked up the multi-hooked squid-jigs and tossed them overside.

Now came rest, and fun.

The boats came close together and the fishermen relaxed.

Tom clambered over to the Andersons' boat to visit skinny Jimmy Anderson, to rub it in about beating him to the coach when the merchant came that time, and to show off the wolverine claw.

There is an old saying, "You'll hear it all on the squid-jigging ground." Those who say only women gossip would laugh to hear the talk when the men sprawled out to rest their weary limbs. Some slept, some yarned, and all talked their fill as they waited for the ten-legged bait.

And it was here that Tom heard of the Island of Black Winds.

"You can see it of a clear morning," said skinny Jimmy Anderson's skinny father, James, "Due east o' Bell Island."

"Ya don't mean Baccalieu, do ya?" asked Tom, who was of course familiar with the local geography, his life depending on it. "Thin line 'gainst the sky, 'bout a six-hour row?"

"No, b'y, not Baccalieu, not the big island. This one is afore that, a leetle one, real small—but oh, me son, the fishin' there! The cod so thick ya hardly can row. They clogs yer oars, too many fish." He nodded, so the blue curl of smoke wavered as it rose from his pipe.

"Well, why don't we go fishin' there?"

Theophilous and Daniel exchanged glances.

James Anderson, Sr., took the pipe from his mouth. "Well, b'y," he said, "is ya eager to meet the horned fella? Old Harry hisself, 'e lives there on the Island of Black Winds," said Old Jim, lean brown face serious as he could get. "'Tis the Devil's summer home."

"You 'lows that can't be true." Tom held a piece of hard-tack overside to soften the rock hard biscuit.

"Have ya never heard the hollies a-callin' in the storm?"

"Well, sure, ever'body knows about hollies," said Tom, glancing carelessly up at the sky, checking on the weather. "They'm spirits."

"Yis, b'y," said James Anderson, "the ghosts o' poor drowned fishermen, ferever wanderin' the sea. And if ya was fool enough to go near that turrible place, you'd hear them at twilight, the voices of the dead callin' out, 'Where to go? Where to go?' an' the answer always comin' back the same . . . 'Jack's in hell, Jack's in hell.'

"And woe to the man who's caught there when the winds of blackness swirl, and the stars an' the moon is gone. Fer then (if the Devil's to home), you'll see his one great eye shinin' through the dark, just afore he snatches ya up, an' then—well, ya don't want to know."

"But . . . is they a *lot* o' fish there?" Tom asked.

"Fish? Why, you could walk upon 'em, thick as flies on a dead deer's nose, they is that many at the Devil's summer home."

"Squid-oh!" someone shouted.

Tom rushed to get back to his boat. He jerked the jigger, felt it twitch, hauled it up.

Through the clear water Tom watched it rise. The squid. For a second Tom thought the monster had come back.

But this squid looked small and *was* small, about fifteen inches long. Brick-red in fury, arms and tentacles flailed, clutching for anything on which to vent its rage. Tom lifted the hook aboard—*Whoosh!* Black ink jetted full in his face. He muttered a word a preacher wouldn't like and shook the squid off the hook. It fell to the floor.

As he slipped the squid jigger back overboard, Tom heard a faint scratching noise down beside his boots.

He looked down. The little squid was biting the wood,

and the tiny beak left gouges.

"Well, we got bait, sure enough," said Dan'l next morning. "All we need now is some fish."

But the cod did not appear. Had they been hunted out of existence? Certainly there were many countries fishing them hard with many new devices, one of which Theo had built himself. It had taken him two years.

It was a cod trap, a new way of fish catching, and the first one tried in the cove. Many leaves and sections of net had been sewn together to make the shape of a box. The box had a floor and walls, but no top. It also had wings spreading out on each side. The fish would swim along these wings, looking for a way through, until they came to the small entry way. That led into the main parlor, the box. Once the fish entered the parlor, they became confused and swam in circles, unable to find their way back out.

When enough fish were inside, the trap was hauled in. That was how it was supposed to work.

One night Tom, Theo, Daniel Squires, and both the skinny James Andersons set out the new cod trap. It was awkward and heavy, with floats on top and lead weights on the bottom, and required help to put in place or haul out.

"I anchored it light as I could," Theo said, "so's the five of us could handle it.

"We'll get a good night's sleep fer once," said Theo. "Come back in the marning; see what our trap caught fer us."

But all they found the next morning was a miserable great chunk of ice. A growler, so-called because of the noise it made grinding up against another ice block, had drifted in, two tons of blue-white trouble following the current around the edge of the cove into the Piccots' cod trap.

It was then, of course, that the cod arrived.

Everybody else was frantically fishing cod, but all Tom and Theo and Daniel could do was try to save their net. They untied and unwrapped the net section by section where they could, chopped with axes where they could not free the net, sometimes standing right on the growler, hacking off the blue-white pieces, working and cursing.

It took two days just to get the net out. It took thirty-seven days—all the rest of June and most of July—to mend the trap, and all that time they had no twine working, no fish being caught to pay off their debt.

They missed the whole spring run of cod.

"Well, there's still the summer run yet, and we've got the best berth in t' cove," said Tom, and even Theo had to agree. The strip of water around the unnamed island was theirs, and the natural movement of the fish was to swim around the island. If the trap was there, they would take cod, no question.

Golden days followed. The heat of summer days could be surprising when it came, but the nights remained foggy and cool, so everyone (who had time to sleep) could get their rest. The green hills never went brown, refreshed by fogs and mists in the night, besprinkled with dew in the morning. And the sea was always changing, yet always the same.

The cod came again, great waves of fish, and now the Piccots' trap began to work. The flick of fins at the surface told them when the trap was full.

They rowed out with dip nets, and quick as a snap they filled their dories with madly flapping cod.

Rowing back, Tom and Daniel used the long fish spears, called pews, to pitch the cod one by one to the stage. The cod must be stabbed in the skull for pitching; a rip in the flesh would lower its value, make it dry wrong.

On the stage, Mark Josephus, Baby Sally, and Lynny carried each cod to the table. Lynny hauled the biggest ones, which might weigh one hundred pounds. But most of the trap fish were small—two, three, ten pounds, members of a school—the lunkers tended to swim alone.

At the table Theo, Ma, and the Widow Crandall cleaned and coarse-salted the cod. Like a river of silver the fish began to move, and until it stopped, nobody stopped.

Pitch the fish. Carry the fish. Slash two cuts along the throat.

Slice the belly, save the liver, toss the guts down the trunk hole.

Break the neck and tear off the body. Kick a few heads aside for later. If you have time, pull off the fish "faces," saving cod cheeks and "tongue" (the underside of the jaw) for a good fish frying; the rest of the heads go through the trunk hole.

Open the cod with a quick slash of blade, taking most but not all of the spine. Leave too much backbone and the blood rots inside; take it all and the fish loses shape when it dries.

Now rub on some salt, stack the flat triangles, and wait for two days.

When the salt had sunk into the fish just enough, someone needing a rest (this was easy work) would take it to the rams-horn, a half-sunken tub in the shallows. There a scrub brush would carefully scour off the white crystal salt that had oozed out the pores. Too much salt "burned" the fish, making it brittle.

When the fish was scrubbed and rinsed, anybody who was free would set the fish out, one by one, to dry in the sunshine.

And every night the fish must be taken up in piles and

covered to protect it from the ever-present possibility of rain. Everyone watched for signs of approaching weather, by which they meant storms. If a cat washed the upper half of its face, some believed that meant rain coming. There were even poems to help predict weather:

If your goats come in measured files,
Stack your fish in covered piles,

one such poem went.

It was not a joke. If the goats just wandered any old way, no reason to worry. But if they lined up so the strongest goat would check the footing, and every other goat walked where the leader judged it safe to step—that meant something.

It took a week of medium sun to cure the fish just right.

That was if you had enough salt.

Theo traded most of their remaining dried cod to get the salt they had to have. When that was gone, Ma traded her four hooked rugs that felt so nice underfoot and looked so pretty. The rugs brought in another quarter barrel of salt, but soon that, too, was gone.

They had to get more salt. Without it they could only do the poor man's cure, just spreading the fish out to sun, unsalted. That meant low-quality cod.

"When you're out o' salt, you're out o' luck," said Theo.

Then Ma said something Tom thought surprising:

"We are the Piccots," she said. "If we has to, we'll make our own luck—and our own salt."

Baby Sally and Mark Josephus, being most easily spared from fish-making, were given the salt-making chores. It did not sound hard: just feed a fire, watch the big iron kettle full of seawater as it boiled, pour in more seawater with the tea can every so often until the stuff in the kettle looked cloudy—a thin, salty syrup called brine. Having no grain salt, they must use this. It would not make the finest quality fish, but it was the best they could do.

Mark Josephus and Baby Sally stacked wood around the kettle by the shoreline. Tom lit the fire. Then he went back to making the fish.

For a while it seemed all right. The littles watched the kettle boil, Baby Sally bringing wood, Mark Josephus adding water with the tea can when the level lowered.

Mark Josephus daydreamed sometimes. He was thinking about school and wishing he could read Tom's book when Baby Sally tripped and fell in the fire.

She screamed but did not wait to be rescued, getting quit of the fire as fast as she could. Her dress and petti-coats were in flames, but she ran out to the waves, dunking the fire.

Ma carried her home, soothed her burns with special cream of winter wood made earlier of mashed-up pulp scraping from a yellow birch's inner bark. She also gave the child a spoonful of rum to make her sleep. Then Ma went back to work, checking up on Baby Sally every couple hours.

"How bad?" asked Theo.

"She'll not be workin' today," Ma snapped. She was so angry it was hard for her not to hurt the fish when she split them. She had to make herself be careful.

The burns were not crippling. Baby Sally's left cheek would be scarred where she'd fallen on the kettle, and her left forearm and right hand were deeply burned where she had pushed herself up from the hot metal and been in contact with it the longest. She had been very lucky. If the kettle had rocked over, the boiling contents would have burned her to death.

Everyone felt miserable about it. Mark Josephus felt bad

because he was the older and in charge, being seven years old now, and he had let his sister get hurt. Theo was ashamed that he had not got more fish in and so his children had to work. Tom hollered at Mark Josephus, which made Lynny yell at Tom. He barked at her, Mark Josephus started to cry, and Ma told them all to shut up. Silence fell.

But the work continued, as it must, if they were not to starve.

One morning in late August a shark entered into Portugal Cove. This was not unusual, of course. Sharks were just scenery most of the time. But this shark was different, an enormous living shadow bending its way south at Sail Point, moving slowly, but unstoppable as time, along the west side of the cove.

Tom saw it from the stage.

"Skipper," he said, "I think there's a basker comin' in t' cove."

"Oh, no," said Theo, understanding instantly. "Is it—to the trap?"

"Get out, get out, you brainless sleveen!" Tom shouted at the shark, not at his father. Frantically the two clambered down the big beam ladder from the stage. Tom ran ahead along the shore; Theo followed quick as he could, heading to the footbridge between landwash and little island. Tom snatched up some rocks on the way.

The intruder was a basking shark, harmless to humans, unless it leaped and fell on your boat, which event would be followed by funerals. The slow-moving shark was enormous, thirty feet of rough-skinned primitive fish. Tom saw its blunt snout and cavernous mouth, glimpsed the white of gill strainers inside like the baleen of a whale. The shark's back was dry from basking in the sun as it swam.

Tom threw rocks and shouted, and he was good at both.

Several of the rocks landed squarely, thudding on the shark's broad rough back. It flinched when the rocks hit but was too stupid to think what to do. Its "brain" was little more than a thickening of spinal column, and the shark kept swimming straight ahead.

In stunned disbelief Tom watched it swim straight into the Piccots' fish trap. The basker barely seemed to notice, at first, as its enormous front accumulated fish trap, layer on layer on layer of carefully handwoven net.

Then the shark turned, in slow acceleration, heading northward from the cove, north and east and down. Doubtless it was trying to escape its new situation, but instead the tangling problem came along.

Tom raced to borrow Ephraim Samuels's harpoon. The older man had been a whaler out of New Bedford for a time and still had his old lily iron hung on the wall of his kitchen. But by the time Tom got back, it was too late.

"I should've anchored the trap heavier," said Theophilous as the great stupid shark disappeared.

The net was gone.

CHAPTER ELEVEN

ISLAND OF BLACK WINDS

◆　　◆　　◆

The Piccots hoped for a time that the net floats would drag the shark and trap to the surface sooner or later. Maybe it did, somewhere. But Conception Bay is very large, and the Atlantic Ocean, well . . .

Pieces of the net were found, reeking with foul glop, a slime that basking sharks have. These torn net leaves were returned. Everyone in the cove knew everybody else, and no one would be mean enough to steal another's work. Net-making styles were individual and could be recognized. But it didn't matter. There wasn't enough material to make the trap again.

The Piccots had no choice but to return to that cheap and ancient fishing method: one man in a dory, two lines, and two hooks apiece.

In separate boats Tom and Daniel worked, one line in each hand, twitching wrists back and forth in the time-honored way to make the lead-weight jigger seem alive, and to catch what fish they could.

Theo worked on his barrels, coopering by feel, stopping only to help make the fish on days when they brought in enough.

Ma and the children helped at other people's stages, working for food.

Everyone brought home what they earned, and Ma cooked whatever it was—half a cod, some molasses, a root-cellared but still good potato, a cup of wheat flour with not too many bugs.

One thing about being busy—the summer flew by. They wished it would go slower, for each passing hour brought them closer to settling-up time.

Last year when they had met with the merchant, they had not had enough to pay their debt. This time they would have still less. If the merchant insisted on being fully paid off, he would ruin them.

The Piccots knew full well what that could mean. The law was on the merchant's side. He might bring the magistrate with him or send for him afterward from St. John's. The magistrate had a little iron hammer, and with it he would nail a piece of parchment to the front door of their house. The paper meant the Piccots no longer owned their home. They could not go inside nor take any of their belongings: not their dories, nor such nets as they had left—nothing. They were allowed only the clothes on their backs, and those would be searched in case they were trying to steal some of their own property.

Where would they go? What could they do? They could not get a job with some other St. John's merchant. The merchants knew each other. They had a gentlemen's agreement to not hire any outporters who owed money to another merchant. If they did, the merchants reasoned, the outporters could work here and there as they wanted and never pay their debts.

Tom heard his parents arguing one night when they thought he was asleep. At first he could not make out what they said in the kitchen several walls away, but one part came through loud and clear.

"We'll just start over somewhere else," Ma said.

"With what?" snapped Theo. "We'll have nothin'!"

"Shush!" Ma said. "You'll fright the childern."

Their voices went low. Tom heard no more, only the worry and the helpless anger.

So one Sunday in late August, after Sunday school and second service, Tom said, "I'm goin' fer a walk, Skipper."

Theophilous said nothing, just sat on the edge of the daybed. He was staring at the kitchen wall and sucking on his empty pipe. Tobacco was long gone. Ma was back behind the house, changing the beds, which meant taking out the eider duck feathers and washing them.

He had not completely lied, Tom figured. He was really going for a walk. He strolled down to the storehouse, and picked up his new-mended sail. Then he walked down to the landwash to his dory, the *Rosie May*.

Murphy, of course, was by his side and hopped eagerly into the dory. Tom grunted and heaved, pushing the heavy wooden dory into the low surf. He was glad for the slippery seaweed now growing over the half-buried slipway.

"Where ya goin', b'y? Fish ain't runnin'," said shriveled-up Mr. McClintock, out with his wife for a dodge along the landwash. "Not t' mention 'tis *Sunday*," added the equally withered Mrs. McClintock, pursing her thin lips.

"I know. I'm just after dogfish fer to feed me animal," said Tom. He did not stop, but pulled the front of his hair same as he'd take off his cap if he had one along. He had no fishing clothes with him. That was part of the plan. He had food and bait stored in the dory, but his oilskins would have been noticed at once if missing from their pegs at the door.

Moving quick as he could, Tom rowed out along the western shore, out toward the mouth of the cove. He flinched as he turned his head and saw his mother in the distance, hanging clothes beside the house.

He hoped Ma did not see him. But there was also a little part of him that hoped she would. In a way, he almost wanted to be caught, to be sent home—in trouble, but safe.

But when he sneaked a look behind him again, ready to duck and pretend he had not seen her, nor heard her if she yelled, there was nobody standing on Grayman's Beard Hill.

Tom reached Sail Point at the edge of the cove and went out into the waves of Conception Bay. It was not hard to tell when he left the wind's shadow coming out from behind the cove's sheltering wall, the half-circle of rock that broke the force of the sea. Here the waves were choppy, and he felt each thump against the hull. He settled to his course, changing his direction, going with the wind.

Now the water lifted, pushed him.

Looking back, he could see the line where calm water began inside the cove where the people were, those who had not broken the Sabbath.

Tom was nervous. He knew the Tickle fairly well, that gap of sea between Portugal Cove and Bell Island. But that was all he knew of Conception Bay, except for a couple trips with Grandfather. He was leaving home waters. He knew he was not fisherman enough for such a trip, not by himself. He did not know where the hidden rocks, called sunkers, were nor the pattern of the currents—which to ride and which to steer wide from.

But the stiff breeze was friendly and in the right direction, due east toward the island, the one just before Baccalieu. Tom set the dory's sail. Then he pushed one oar behind him out the stern notch. He would oar-scull with one hand, work the sail with the other. If need be, he could rig a rope to let him sail with one foot and free both hands for sculling.

"Baccalieu just means cod," he said, more to himself than to Murphy. "And cod's what I'm wantin', so that's where I'll go."

He almost did not need to steer. The wind caught his pocket of sail, and he raced along with Murphy standing in the bow, seeming to enjoy the ride. If the wind kept up and the waves kept helping, Tom thought, he could reach the island in four hours.

The trick would be getting home. He hoped the winds would shift in late afternoon as they had the past three days. If they did, he could ride the waves the whole way, smooth and easy like now. If not, well, he would have to row home.

"Git me the grub sack, will ya, Murphy?" said Tom. "'Tis in the forward cuddy, as well ya know."

The cuddy was a small covered area in the front of the boat. There Tom kept his tomahawk, grub sack, bait, odds and ends of gear. The cuddy was large enough to crawl partly under in case you wanted to sleep there in a storm.

Murphy brought over the food sack. Tom did not puzzle much how the dog knew what he wanted. Peggeen had told him Newfoundland dogs have bigger brains. Tom did not know or care about that. He just knew he could talk to Murphy, and, as long as he talked slow and simple, the big black dog seemed to understand.

For Tom there were three pieces of bread, hard ship biscuit. Tom dunked one chunk overside, softening it with the salt water, and began to chew. The nice thing about hardtack was it chewed practically forever. There were also a dozen partly dried capelin for Murphy, who disposed of them with appreciative crunching.

Tom thought about the scar on Baby Sally's cheek. It had healed crooked, tugging down the corner of one eye. Ma told her it looked good, like a pirate or something, and in truth it did not spoil her looks. Ma had Lynny rub cod oil on the back of Baby Sally's knee, so the scar would grow back flexible, not tighten and draw the flesh together, make her limp. Her hand could close pretty well now, and the other forearm gave no trouble as it healed. But she'd carry those scars to the end of her life.

If only he could go back and do things over.

All his fault. If he hadn't blabbed about the woodsdevil so much, it might not have heard them, never come to their tilt in the forest. Theo wouldn't have shot off the rifle and got half-blind when the gun blew up. And if Tom hadn't fought with the merchant's brat, their credit wouldn't be cut off now. They'd have had their own salt, ready-made, not needing any homemade brine. Baby Sally would not have been tending the kettle. She would not have fallen into the fire. Skipper and Ma wouldn't be worryin' about losing their home. . . .

"'Tis all my doin'. I got to fix it," he said aloud. Murphy came back to him and put his big head on Tom's thigh.

He knew he would be in trouble when he got home.

Fishing on the Sabbath, that was serious. Might even get whipped like that one time before.

But the wind from the west felt warm on his back.

If he got in trouble later, well, that was for later, not now. He had done what he thought was right to do. A man has to make his decisions, he thought, and then stand beside them, pay the price. He was looking out for his family the best way he knew how. It was dangerous and stupid and against the Sunday law. But he was going.

He remembered Grandfather. Surprisingly, he did not feel guilty anymore. Grandfather would understand, he thought. Just for a second he remembered the old man so strong it was as if the tan, weathered hand rested on his shoulder. Tom smiled and blinked.

The *Rosie May* gained speed. The winds were picking up.

Hunger dulled, Tom tossed the sack back in the cuddy, made his stomach produce a glorious belch, and then began to sing.

Now, Tom really loved to sing, in church or out. His voice might lack some in beauty, but it sure had plenty of loud. He sang what he could remember of the National Anthem, "Ode to Newfoundland."

And then he sang some more.

He even sang, "Oh hear us when we call to Thee, for those in peril on the sea." But then he wished he hadn't, for this was a funeral song for when a boat went down and the bodies were never recovered.

The sea beneath him was smooth but rising, as though he rode the back of some great animal that had not noticed him yet. Weatherbreeder, he thought. Storm's comin' on. How long did he have till it broke? Grandfather would have known. Theo would know. Tom studied the sky, shook his head, and went on.

Hours passed without trouble. The sun had traveled; so had Tom. The sky was copper-gold and red where it showed through the darkening clouds. The winds were alive and chasing.

And before Tom rose the Island of Black Winds.

It did not look frightening. Just a great huge rock, maybe a hundred feet tall, three-quarters of a mile long, covered with birds.

Yellow-beaked, orange-footed, black-and-white puffins all together at one side; tiny sea swallows, called petrels, surrounded patches of long-necked gannets on the other. The petrels made strange noises, almost like words. Sea gulls scavenged everywhere. So many birds, the roar of their noise like the sound of the surf.

The dark cliffs were white with droppings. Bird dirt, Tom thought, as he caught a whiff and wished he hadn't. "Dang!" he said, "that's powerful!"

Beyond this island was another, larger—Baccalieu Island—a few miles away. At one end of that, Tom could see a tall white tower, windows of glass glimmering at the top.

"Must be one o' them *lighthouses,*" Tom said. "What a fine thing, to warn folks off the rocks by night." He had seen a lighthouse before at Fort Amherst, by The Narrows to the harbor at St. John's.

He took down his sail, needing caution, not speed. Even so the breeze took him nearer and nearer. A wave broke white, flowering across sharp rock. The wavewash made a greedy sucking sound.

"Might be a good ledge nigh that sunker," Tom said. "Fish favor a rock wall. Don't know why. Calm spot, I s'pose, or maybe a current turns up at the wall, brings 'em food. Anyways, we'll try berthin' here."

Anchoring his boat with the kellick, Tom baited his hooks with half-rotten squid and tossed the two lines overside.

The dory raised and lowered with the sea.

The setting sun bathed all in gold and red and orange.

The wind pushed harder, like a hand on his boat, so it strained against the anchor rope.

Then the winds shifted, coming now from the island. The whipping gusts carried something in them, something that made Tom's eyes water and burn, filled his mouth and nostrils, and made him fight for breath.

"I guess this must be the black winds," Tom said, squinching his eyes to a slit. "Smells like bird dirt to me, nothin' magic 'bout that, just hard t' see is all."

But then the fish began to strike. Tom yanked and hauled, and a fat cod came flopping over the side. Ahh. How fine that fish looked to him. He thought about the debt and Baby Sally needing milk.

But now the cod came too quick for thought, and fast as he could clear each hook and get it overside, the next fish came. He fished and fished, and the line whipped through his fingers, cutting, but he paid no mind to the blood; it was just some more wetness in the swirling dusk.

He fished and fished and fished until the run stopped.

When the cod moved away, or maybe lost interest, the *Rosie May* was low in the water, her gunwale edges nearly level with the sea. Tom was glad the fish had stopped biting. He could not have made himself quit catching, though it was not safe to be so overloaded.

One full third of the catch was Murphy's contribution. Again and again, without needing to be told, the dog had gone overboard to bring back loose-hooked fish.

"Look how much we got, full to the gunnels," Tom told

Murphy proudly. True, it would shrink to half that when dried, but he had won. He had food to take on home.

And speaking of which, he had best get home right now, ride the winds to the cove before the storm closed in.

The winds hushed, but the stillness did not make him happy. It was like the pulling back of a fist before a blow. He blinked and wiped his eyes clear, smelled the blood from his hands as it got on his face. It startled him for a moment. He thought his nose was bleeding.

Then in the stillness he heard them: voices in the sky.

CHAPTER TWELVE

A CAP OF WIND

◆　　　◆　　　◆

"**W**here to go? Where to go? Where to go?"

And the answer came back just as he'd been told. "Jack's in hell! Jack's in hell!"

The darkness split, and the Devil's Eye blazed down on him. Tom clamped his eyes shut, saw red glare through his eyelids. The Devil was home and would take him away for fishing on a Sunday!

Any second now the blazing claws would clutch around him, pierce him like a carrot on the fork; any second now he'd feel—

A cold nose poking into his hand? "Don't bother me now, Murphy. Can't you see I'm busy gettin' kilt?" said Tom.

The white light left him. Around him were the normal

noises of a rising sea. Curiousity itched. Tom wondered what the Evil One looked like.

But when he sneaked a peek, the blaze returned. He tightened his eyes against it and this time kept them shut. Oh, my, the Devil might ha' missed him! The light blazed and darkened. Blazed and darkened. Something was not right.

He opened his eyes cautiously. The light was not so bright as he had thought. It came not from this island but the one just behind it. From Baccalieu.

The lighthouse?

He had no time to think about it. The wind had shifted. The changing mood of the ocean would not be ignored. He must get home. Tom hauled the anchor.

He dug through the pile of still-wriggling fish, found the sail, and raised it. Adjusting the canvas to the wind's new direction, Tom set the sculling oar in the water and turned the boat around. The light was on his back now, and the winds blew the dust of bird dirt that gritted on the thwart when he moved.

The lighthouse.

That was all it was. He almost laughed, then caught himself.

What about the dead sailors' voices? He listened again.

Jack chack jack where to go chack erell jack in hell, chackerell. Now that he was calmer, it sounded not so much like the voices of the dead but rather like, like— birds. The sea swallows, or petrels, or whatever they were.

Devil's summer home! He'd have to pull some very good trick on James Anderson, the older one, to get even on him.

He put his hand on Murphy's broad back.

"Time we was gettin' home," he said. "We've done a

piece o' work this day, I'll be bound."

Murphy looked beyond the heap of fish to the dark and rising sea between them and home.

"Nothin' t' be worryin' about, Murphy, me son! We'll go home easy as we come. Don't ya feel the wind a-shiftin'?"

But the waves built by the earlier wind still swept on by, lifting and dropping his boat as they went. The gusts of changing breeze behind him were mere twists of air, fickle and uncertain. They had no power and did not last.

Even as he spoke, the breeze that brought him here returned, and strongly. He tacked across the wind at an angle for a time, but was losing more ground than he gained. He lowered the sail and secured it under the piled-up fish. He would have to row.

He had been four hours from home. But how long now, against the wind?

Maybe he should go back behind the little island, stay in the sheltering lee of it? Quick as the thought came, the memory of the sunkers cancelled it. Just one sharp rock could rip the hull of the *Rosie May* and end the voyage for him, permanent. Send him down. With the kraken. No. He could make it. He had to.

Betwixt him and home there was deep water, as long as he kept well back from the coast. He would have to trust his boat.

Clearing the fish away from the middle thwart, Tom seated himself, set the oars between the tholepins, worked his feet down through the cod, and began. He would row facing forward, not keep twisting his neck all around.

Row. Shoulder and stomach muscles contracted as he leaned forward, thrusting the oar blades, then back on the rest stroke, then forward again. His body was not so strong this way, facing front, but at least he could see and adjust to the changes in the water as they came.

Up the building fronts of waves, and down. This was not so bad. He could do this. He was strong.

"We'll just row all night, Murphy, me son, an' show up in the marning wi' the greatest load o' fish in all t' cove."

As his body shifted into the long monotony of labor, his mind tried to drift into the pleasant warmth of memories.

Tom's right oar missed a stroke, the blade skipping across the dark face of a wave. He grew conscious of his surroundings again, saw how the waves were piling and the wind was drawing spindrift from the tops. Up and up the dory climbed, over, and down into the trough.

As he went down he saw the wave ahead, saw a large shark above him, suspended in the water column. The shark swam toward him. Tom's boat lifted. The shark disappeared. Tom expected to feel the rasp of rough hide on the hull, but did not.

Cold wind sapped his strength, chilling neck and hands. He kept the insides of his arms tight to his sides when he could, hugging each instant of warmth. He shivered, wished he'd worn something else besides Sunday clothes. Ma was not gonna like his good clothes all fishy.

Around him stretched the gray Atlantic. It slept no more.

Each storm has its own set of characteristics and is different from every other. This storm seemed dark and puckish at first, playful, full of tricks and misdirections, hints of fearful possibilities. . . .

Then the roaring began, like monsters stalking through the night.

A bolt of lightning. At the top of a wave, Tom saw the protruding tail of a humpback whale, white on the underside, scalloped on the edges. The whale was not diving, just upside down, resting, riding out the storm or maybe playing with it.

A shoal of black pot heads, pilot whales, passed by, leaping directly into the waves of the storm, taking it head on just as Tom did.

He was glad he did not get seasick. He had never been seasick, not once in his life. Why was he thinking about being seasick? he wondered as a wave struck the bottom of the dory with a sickening smash and his stomach lifted and fell. Don't think about it, he remembered telling the preacher's son once, when that person had come out in his boat to see what it was like. Don't think about it. He realized now what foolish advice this had been. How could you ignore the leaping, twisting knot of your guts as it tried to crawl out of your throat?

But he did not vomit, did not let the food come up, although it tried. There wasn't much inside him, and what came up he swallowed back down.

Like a leaf in the wind he went on, into the night and into the storm.

Hours passed uncounted; Tom rowed exhausted. He would die if he quit, so he kept going.

"Oh, Lord," he mumbled in the fisherman's prayer, "Thy sea is so great, and my boat is so small."

The flat-bottomed dory was stable and low, denying the wind a high surface to tip.

Then a crash of cold. An arm of foam slashed over, took a fish.

"No!" he shouted without thought. The words were barely out of his mouth before he realized the muscles bunching beside him were Murphy's, crouching for the leap overboard to rescue the fish and surely die. Once overboard in this, he could not return.

"No, no, don't, don't go in the water! You stay here, Murphy! Stay here wi' me!" Tom yelled, praying the big dog would understand.

A rush of water droplets hurled against his face. It was just spray, he told himself. Not rain. Please, don't let it be rain. It'll cross up the waves.

Lightning. White jagged energy illuminated an eternity of heaving waves and black, boiling clouds. The thunder-crack followed almost instantly.

Every bit of Tom's awareness focused on the tips of his oars, pulling, grabbing for stability in the crashing liquid. Then came the rain, driving sideward, thick and choking, smashed against him by the wind.

Tom had once said he *liked* a good storm, but now he knew that was a lie. He only liked the storm when safe from it, when he could hear the roar outside thick walls, and him inside, warm.

Not like now, his body stiff and wet and aching in cold, fingers numb and nerveless, each breath a struggle, the droplets hitting hard like bursting rocks. Every crash and echo resounded through his head, and Murphy beside him was the only warm thing in the world.

Tom cursed and did not hear the swear. Rain and tears poured down his face; which was which he could not tell.

Wave tops smashed across the bow and in passing took his fish—his fish!—back to the sea. He wanted to stop and bail out the boat, but feared to let go his oars.

Weakness chilled his arms; exhaustion crept into his back.

But never mind. Never mind. Just lean and heave with the shoulders and hands and don't give up. Don't give up. The waves still had a pattern, something to be figured out and to be ridden.

All he had to do was row and row, just keep rowing.

The waves were hungry now, following close behind each other. He could barely deal with one before the next was on him.

He began to count the oar strokes he could get in the front of each wave: one, two—over the top of the wave and down. Down, down—oops, here comes the next. Up, up—*crashhshshsh*—he thought he heard a different sound, the beat of waves on rocky shore. Yes, again! But was it a cliff to break his boat or a rocky shore for safety?

He tried to recognize the rote, the distinctive pattern of wave crash music, pounding on the shore.

For a moment he let himself believe it was his own sweet Portugal Cove. But it was not. The wind was too strong, not gentled as it would have been by his home cove's sheltering hills. This crash of wave on rock was louder, hollow-booming, as though it slammed against an inward arching cliff—Bell Island? That made sense.

He remembered now a hiss he had automatically pulled back from, knowing it meant waves parting around a sharp-edged point of rock—that might have been Old Harry's Point, the tip of the tongue in the clapper of the bell, the bell-shaped rock that gave Bell Island its name.

A light. He saw a little light swinging back and forth. Oh, no. No, it could not be. Had he been blown back, all the way to the Devil's summer house? No! He was off course, he knew, but the natural compass inside his head could not be *that* confused.

He rowed for the light, rowed and rowed, lost progress in the backwash and pulled harder, knowing it was this chance or none. He hoped the light was something real, and nothing that an exhausted brain might just dream up. Then a great wave lifted, flung him. He struck something hard, heard gravel grind beneath, thought he had caught a sunker and was being torn apart. Maybe he had hit a cliff? He looked up.

He was staring at a human face.

"You all right?" said the man with the lantern, leaning into Tom's boat.

"Me fish," said Tom, sitting there in his boat, rocking on the gravel as the water sucked away. His shoulder twitched as if he still rowed.

"What are you doing out here in the middle of the night?" asked the stranger. He had a fisherman's beard and a wart to the right of his nose. His voice was kindly.

"Is I—to Bell Island?" Tom wondered if he were dreaming. Nobody lived on Bell Island. Maybe he had died and was in the Other Place.

"Let's get your boat up; we'll talk later."

"Me fish, got to clean me fish."

"What fish?"

"Well, me—" Tom said, and stopped.

Except for himself and his dog, the boat was empty.

CHAPTER THIRTEEN

WHEN WAKES THE KRAKEN

◆　　　◆　　　◆

T here was a deal of talk, of course, when Tom sailed home in the morning.

First Ma nearly crushed the life out of him, hugging him so hard.

Lynny yelled at him the loudest, perhaps having been the most frightened. He couldn't really hear what she said because she was talking too loud. After a while, when she appeared to have run out of breath, Tom hugged her and smoothed away the tears of fright.

Little Mark Josephus folded his forearms and frowned like the minister. "'Twas a sin to go fishin' of a Sunday," he said.

Tom agreed. "An' foolish, too," he added.

Mrs. McClintock came rushing over to inquire if Tom

had been properly whipped yet. Tom heard his mother say no, but that he had almost drowned, and perhaps that was punishment enough.

"Nosy ol' bag," Tom muttered, not quite low enough for Mrs. McClintock to miss. Not hard to figure who had come and told on him almost as soon as he had left the cove. Theo and Dan'l had taken the other dory and gone out looking for him, searching till the dark and the storm closed in and they could no longer see. Tom felt pangs of real regret as he imagined how helpless and worried they had been.

"I'm sorry, Skipper," he said. "An' I didn't even bring home fish!"

But his father only sighed and shook his head. "A bit airsome out there, wasn' it?" was all he said. Theo was a fisherman. He knew what Tom had been through—his first storm alone on the sea.

Baby Sally said, "Pick me up!" and put her good cheek on Tom's shoulder, kissed him on his neck, and wouldn't let him put her down for a long time.

Mark Josephus unfolded his arms. "Tell about the birds again," he said.

But what nobody could figure was what the strangers had been doing on Bell Island. There had been three of them, Tom remembered, the bearded man who spotted him and held the lamp to guide him in, and two other men, younger, who looked to the man with the beard before they said anything to Tom. They had all taken shelter in a sort of canvas tarp on poles. They called it a tent, and it was noisy, flapping like crazy in the wind till he thought it would blow away. The strangers had their blankets sewn together into padded bags, and the bearded man made Tom take his. He even gave Tom a clean, dry set of folded longjohns, bright red and practically new, and himself hung Tom's soaked clothes on sticks to dry overnight—or at least get a bit less wet—and had snorted when he saw Tom had been fishing in church clothes.

Tom had climbed into one of the "sleeping bags" and never thought to ask whose bed he had taken. How wonderful it had been, to be dry and warm again and to not have to fight the waves. He wakened briefly just before dawn. He heard the three men snoring like loggers and saw the bearded man asleep beneath a pile of clothes.

In the morning they gave him a hen's egg fried in butter. When they saw how fast he ate it, the men looked at each other and fried two more for him.

"Weren't no seabird's egg neither," said Tom. "I never tasted anythin' so good. 'Cept Ma's cookin'," he added hastily.

"They was fishermen, you say?" asked Theo.

"The old feller wi' the beard was, seemed like. I ain't sure 'bout the others."

"But they didn't have no gear along?" put in Noddy Weathers, who had dropped by to discuss the matter.

"Just a lot o' junk I couldn't see no reason for—jam jars an' the like."

"Jam jars?" asked Ma.

Tom nodded. "An' also somethin' like fish-weighin' scales, only small."

"Should have gived the man back his longjohns," said Ma, nodding at the red sleeve poking out from under Tom's church shirt.

"I was goin' to, but he said they was a extry set and he had a son of his own back to home, so don't mind 'bout it."

Ma nodded slowly, the way she did when she made up her mind.

"You go git them folks, Theophilous," said Ma. "Bring them back fer dinner. The least we can do, a kind man like that."

Tom and Theo went across the Tickle to Bell Island, but the men were gone. All that remained were the ashes of their fire.

Noddy Weathers had seen a schooner nearby—was it theirs? Old Mr. McClintock said mayhap they was angels, sent to give foolish Tom a second chance. Not that he deserved it, fishing on Sunday, added Mrs. McClintock.

The Sunday fishing incident became in time a useful lesson in what *not* to do, and Tom was lectured on the subject by almost everybody in the village.

The days went by. Summer winds grew harsh and edged with cold. The Piccots caught more fish. Theo made more barrels.

Settling-up day with the merchant drew nearer and nearer.

And then one morning early, on the twenty-sixth day of October, year of our Lord eighteen seventy-three . . .

"No room for ya this marnin', Murphy," said Theophilous to Tom's dog, who had just jumped into the dory as the men turned the boat and dragged it toward the sea. "Whoosht! Off about yer business now!" Theo made a shooing motion with his hands.

The dog looked at his master. Tom nodded. Only then did the big dog jump from the boat into the shallows by the slipway. And then he immediately turned around and looked at Tom, hoping for a change in plans.

Tom knew his dad was right, of course. The dory would be too crowded: three men, the heaped-up piles of patched net, plus all the fish they intended to catch. But still he had the oddest sick feeling in his stomach, as if he were leaving his good luck behind and might never see Murphy again.

"Hop in, Tom, yer dog'll be glad fer the day off from work," said Daniel Squires, steadying the floating rowboat, half again the size of Tom's. The *Rosie May*, on the slipway beside them, looked forlorn as Murphy, as if it, too, were alive and wanting to go along. Tom clambered to the forward oars of Theo's boat, which was called the *HTW*. That stood for Hot Tempered Woman, for reasons Theo would not explain. Tom had put the letters on, he being the family writer.

Theo and Daniel shoved, then hopped in themselves. The dory settled under their weight and glided out.

On the landing, Murphy turned away.

"Murphy?" Tom said half under his breath.

Instantly the dog was back at the edge of the slipway again, ready to jump in the water and swim after the boat. Theo glanced at his son.

"Stay, boy," Tom said.

And Murphy's face growing smaller was the last thing Tom saw as they rowed from the cove and into the mist.

As the fog swirled around them Tom heard a small sound seeming not quite right for where they were. A harbor noise. The whispering flap of sailcloth, creak of wood, and taut ropes straining. And the rush of something moving through the water.

"Starboard, fer yer lives!" yelled Theo. Frantically they rowed, yanking the boat violently to the right.

A great clipper ship burst through the mist. They were lifted by its bow wave, saw the high wooden sides with covered porthole doors for cannon, and beyond that tall masts and canvas sails. Two sailors on deck were looking down. One pointed and laughed; the other only grabbed his beard and stared wide-eyed at them.

"She'd a-crushed us, sure," said Dan'l, who was shaking.

"Didn't seem they'd care too much, s'posin' they did run us down," said Tom.

"'Tis the merchant's ship," said Theo, "come fer settlin' up. Guess squarin' up time's here tomarrow, I hoped we'd git a few more days."

They rowed on in the fog.

"Skipper?" said Tom.

"Ahrr?"

"How we goin' to do tomarrow? At the settlin' up, I mean."

"Dunno, boy."

"How much do ya owe?" asked Daniel Squires.

"Hunnert fourteen pounds, ten shillin'." Theo sighed.

"And how much ya figger they'll give us fer our quintals o' dry fish?" asked Tom.

"Depends how strict they cull, an' what price they sets. If they was fair, might be hunnert pounds or more," said Theo.

"Which leaves us owin' how much?" Tom wanted to know.

"I ain't sure. You'm the one that's been to school."

Subtraction was a third-year skill, and Tom had quit school after second.

"Think they'd give that much fer them good barrels ye made?" Daniel asked.

"If they is fair about it, which I mistrust."

"Should be enough," said Dan'l.

Tom remembered the nights he had come home from lobster fishing to find Theo sawing wood by flickering lamplight, the half-blind man struggling to be exact with each cut, wrestling with a saw meant for two men. Theo just thought it was natural that a man should do whatever it took to keep his family safe.

"So why is we out fishin' if we've got enough?" asked Tom. He too was tired. The thought of bed, of snuggling under the warm eiderdown comforter, shutting his eyes, just doing *nothing*—that seemed like an impossible dream.

"Because there's no way o' knowin' will they give us a fair price," said Daniel, figuring Theo was tired of talk.

Tom held his breath for a minute, then blinked, bit his lower lip, and said, "Skipper?"

"What now?"

Tom judged the risk, accepted it, and went on. "Somethin' have been troublin' me. I don't know how to say it exactly, but—well, is what happens tomarrow wi' the merchant all set out fer us? Like there is some big book have it writ do we live or die? So we could look ahead an' know do the debt get paid off an' we gets food fer the winter."

"Ya means like the debt log, the fat, heavy book the merchant keeps?" asked Daniel Squires. He was steering today, seated at the back.

"I seen that book," said Theo at the middle oars. "All that ink what catches us, like a net made out o' words."

"No, no," said Tom. "I don't mean a real book."

"Then how do ya mean, b'y?" asked Daniel.

Tom wrestled with the thought a second. Except for Theo, nobody minded idle talk on a long row. It helped to pass away the time. They were already well past Greeley's Hill and Oar's Deep, where Tom had seen the beast.

"I mean, is ever'thin' already set do we win or lose?" he said.

"Yis, b'y," said Daniel. "I think so. See, I knowed two boys once, good fishermen both. On'y one could swim, and t' other couldn't. They got caught in some weather, a patch o' wind, airsome fer certain. Boat turned over. The one as could swim? He drowned. The one as could *not* swim, he lived. It wasn' his time to die, that's all. When 'tis yer time, ya dies, nothin' ya can do 'bout it."

"Them's my feelin's," agreed Theo shortly.

"And 'tis good in a way," said Daniel. "We don't have to worry, 'cause if we live or die is already set, an' nothin' we can do about 'er."

"Then why do we work so hard?" Tom had been puzzling on this. "If 'tis all set down an' goin' to happen anyway, why can't we just lean back an' let 'er happen."

Theo spoke up.

"'Cause that's wrote down, too, in that big pre-tend book o' yours, how things is meant to be. It's all set down do we like it or not. We works on a dory, while the fat merchant boy sleeps in on the clipper. 'E's rich all 'is life, we'm poor fer all ours. That's how 'tis," said Theophilous, straining to see through the fog with his half-ruined eyes.

"But I can't believe that," said Tom. "Seems to me like—*we* should do the writin' of our lives. Like Peggeen told me one time, she said, 'Just 'cause things *is* don't mean they is right.' Maybe we can fix things, make 'em better, like you done wi' the net when she was brung back in rags. You didn't say, oh, well, she's ruined, let's toss 'er. No, you fixed her. And—"

The men never knew what Tom might have said next.

"Looky there!" said Daniel Squires.

Before them in the mist was something huge and mixed-color, purplish and white. It was half-floating and, like an iceberg, there seemed to be more underneath. Even the part they could see was bigger than the twenty-foot dory.

"A scuttled ship! She's ours!" said Theo. "Salvage rights! Overturned ship belongs t' the first man that finds 'er. We can sell 'er, pay our debt fer certain sure. This is luck fer us, b'ys!"

"That ain't no ship," said Daniel Squires.

"Kraken," said Tom. "It's yer kraken, big squid like I seen before." His chest shook, breath came in short gasps. His hands looked like chalk where they gripped the front oars. "Don't mess with he! Think on Bill Darling and the schooner *Pearl* that was pulled down."

"Be easy, son," said Theo. "If 'tis a squid, which I misdoubt 'cause I never seen no thing so big, he must be dead, long gone, else why'd he be up here in almost broad daylight, hidin' in the mist? Whatsomever he was, he is ours now," said Theo as he picked up the boathook.

As if time slowed, Tom watched his father raise the gaff. Such a small, unimportant move, it seemed. The human hand gripping the long wooden handle, the metal hook rising in a short arc. Theo hesitated for one split second.

"Don't do it," whispered Tom.

Thunk! The gaff sank into the purplish mass.

And the sleeping kraken woke.

They heard a *whooshshsh* as volumes of water sucked in under the edges of the hood of the beast.

Then it rose tailfirst, so the flaring tip of it was thirty feet above the water, and the monster looked down at them.

Tom's eyes raised. His head went back.

It was so big, rising higher from the water than their house was tall on land. Everything about it seemed wrong and strange, as if the creature was built upside down: wide, flaring tailfin on top, then the smooth enormous streamlined body—head and huge eyes at the middle—and under that the legs—so many! Like a purple-white forest.

Then it changed color: purplish white rippling to orange, to pink, to pure cream white, and darkening at last to the deep brick red of rage.

The four-foot-long boathook looked small where it

hung, suspended in the side of the giant squid's head, the wooden handle dangling down beside huge, staring eyes. Then the face, if such it could be called, twitched once. The offending object flipped away. Green blood oozed where the boathook had torn the flesh.

Something like a great fingerless hand rose dripping from the water. The white underside of it writhed, alive with dozens of moving circles—suction cups—and each one edged with tiny jagged teeth.

The hunting tentacle hissed through the air. A crack and a splash, and Tom's end of the dory was completely encircled by the long narrow tentacle and clutching hand.

Another arm reached toward the middle of the boat. This limb did not have the leaf-shaped grabber on the end but was thick like a big man's thigh. Slightly pointed at the tip, it moved with grace and cunning, with little twitching ripples side to side, a monstrous fumbling thing. Sharp-edged suction disks showed in a double row on the under-side.

It gripped. Tom saw long ropes of muscle flex across the arm, heard the splintering crack of wood tearing.

Then the monster leaned down to examine what it held.

An eye, bigger than Tom's whole head, came close to him. The eye was like a black, dead shield, ringed in white. The glisten on its surface reflected his frightened face. He could read no expression in that huge, dark eye, no hint of emotion; just eternal coldness, endless night. Then the eye flashed that hideous, remembered green.

The boat shifted. Other arms, heavy and thick, moved to secure it, taking control.

Theo snatched up an oar, swung it with all his might.

There was a meaty thump. Then the oar was flicked from Theo's grasp. Blazing green-black eyes studied the oar, then brought it near the water.

Something like a fleshy curtain rippled back. Tom gasped. He saw the beak emerge at the monster's underside, lunging from its fleshy sheath in a white space at the middle of the arms.

The beak was dark brown, edged with black, big as a six-gallon barrel. It rotated slightly, reaching the appropriate angle. It opened. He saw the strange, rough, black tongue, like a flexible file. It rasped on the oar, tasting it. Tom remembered the empty lobster he had found with its insides all licked out.

The beak crunched together. A cracking snap, and the broken oar was pitched aside, rejected as inedible.

Tom's gaze was fixed on that iron-hard beak. It was like a sailor's parrot's beak, he thought, but the lower half was bigger than the top. My head could fit inside there, he thought, looking into the mouth of darkness. The rough-edged radular tongue emerged again, this time to reach and rasp the gunwale edge of the boat.

Then the beak emerged farther and twisted, bit, took a notch from the boat's wooden gunwale edge right beside the oarlock. The beak opened. The piece of wood dropped out.

The kraken tensed. The dory began to lower, at first straight down, slowly. It was not easy. Would the creature tire of the process, just snatch them off the boat, leaving it to drift ashore without them, no one to ever know how they died? The slow descent continued.

The monster shifted its weight. One side of the dory went under, breaking the surface tension. Water rushed aboard. Even through his boots Tom felt the cold.

From habit Daniel Squires began to bail, shoveling out water with the wooden bailing bucket called the piggin.

Then he stopped, half-laughed at the ridiculousness of it—trying to bail as the boat was being dragged under. Cold liquid rose to their ankles, to their shins.

Daniel Squires nodded to Tom, then grinned at Theo, his friend for so many years. "God be wi' ya," he said, the old-fashioned way of saying good-bye.

Theophilous nodded. His broad shoulders slumped. He tried to see his son, then looked down. They had done their best, and failed.

Time to die.

Then Tom Piccot went a little bit crazy. "NOOOO!"

Unblinking giant eyes turned toward him as Tom leaped to the forward cuddy, fumbling inside the boat's storage compartment.

For one awful second he could not find what he searched for—and then Tom's fingers closed around the handle of the bait ax.

"Ya heathen beast!" he screamed.

Tom swung the tomahawk, hard as he'd ever chopped wood, on the long hunting tentacle that held his end of the boat. The hand ax cut pale flesh. Green blood flowed. Tom hit again, missing, then connected, cutting right through the arm into the wood underneath.

He went berserk, attacking anything that was not boat or net or men. Shrieking curses and threats, he chopped—*Whack! Whack! Whack!* In a mad rush he clambered back and forth across the boat, one end to the other, fighting all the way, though he missed far more than he hit. He thumped one moving arm in the air again and again, accomplishing nothing, like chopping a tree that wouldn't hold still. But one arm he caught where it crossed the gunwale, and that he cut through in one clean chop. The stub of severed limb whipped back, part of its alien length still aboard.

Suddenly the situation changed.

As the spider yanks back burnt limbs from the fire, the squid retracted what was left of its arms. The sea turned black for hundreds of yards as the squid shed ink in its own fear.

In fingersnap quickness, the giant squid slid under the boat. Even through the ink, its enormous bulk and length could be seen beyond the dory on both sides. Was it sixty feet long? Or eighty? Bigger than a whale.

The kraken surfaced on the other side.

"Come here, I'll chop off yer head!" yelled Tom.

"Hush, don't make it mad!" said Daniel.

Theo stood up and grabbed Tom. With a great heave of strength Theophilous lifted him, moved him to the back, and took his place to row. Tom barely noticed. He kept on yelling, but Daniel snatched the sculling oar from behind him and jumped to the middle bench.

Putting the stern oar in place of the one that was gone, Daniel started to row with Theo.

"I'll tear out yer liver!" yelled Tom at the squid.

The men rowed as if they had gone wild. The squid followed close, swift and agile, hurtling under, around, before and behind them, like a self-guiding arrow.

"I'll cut ya t' fish bait. I'll rip out yer pips!" Tom yelled. "Pips" was not nasty, just another word for squid guts. Tom was running low on insults suitable for giant squid.

They passed Oar's Deep, neared Greeley's Hill. Racing for the cove, the men rowed smooth and swift.

"Come on, come on, I'll kill youuuuu!" yelled Tom.

The kraken flashed under, then reared up before them, tall as the biggest building in St. John's. They saw the great triangle fins at the tail of the giant squid; just the tail alone looked ten feet across.

Green-black eyes blazed down into Tom's. He went silent, awed.

He stared and stared, hard as he could. The creature slipped beneath the surface, and the water rushed together in a quiet *shhloop* where the giant squid had been.

CHAPTER FOURTEEN

THE DAY OF RECKONING

◆   ◆   ◆

T*hunk. Thunk.* The tomahawk chopped on the giant squid's arm. What a strange kind of flesh it was, strong as leather, soft as jelly. Even dead across the chopping stump, the arm of the devilfish seemed almost alive.

Thinking Ma could stew it or something, Tom put a small raw chunk in his mouth. Bitter fluid squeezed out of the meat in his teeth. The longer he chewed it, the worse it got. It smelled like fish, but it tasted like—like—ugh.

He spat it on the ground. Murphy looked up as if to ask, Are you finished with that? Tom nodded. The chunk of squid disappeared. Tom continued to spit, trying to get rid of the taste in his mouth. Murphy studied the rest of the squid arm intently.

"Yis, b'y," Tom said, "much as ya wants." He fed Murphy

until the dog belched, lay down, and turned his head away. By now other dogs had gathered, and Tom fed Skinner, Charley, and Ahab, who had worked so hard on the team. Daniel Squires always gave them any food he could spare, but that was not much. Mostly the dogs scavenged for themselves, eating food they could find.

Tom threw the rest of the arm to the gathering of dogs. Instantly there was a snarling tug of war. Anything torn off was swallowed so its owner could go back and fight for more. If the piece was too large to get down at once, the animal ran off with it, followed by growling others.

Tom picked up part of the second squid arm, the long hunting tentacle. This was different from the other—thin throughout most of its length, ending in a wider section, that enormous fingerless hand, bigger than Tom.

Dog eyes watched the food intently. Slobber dripped from exposed teeth.

Thunk. Thunk. Thunk. Tom chopped off the giant squid's hand at the narrow wrist and coiled the rest on the woodpile.

"Tom, Tom, wait!" came a voice faintly.

Tom looked up. Why was Daniel Squires running so fast? Behind Daniel was their minister, Pastor Gabriel, who gave such wonderful long sermons. Tom had never seen him run before. And Theo, too, was running beside him, best as he could. Bad eyes gave Theo problems with balance so that he weaved side to side, as if he was drunk.

"Where is the squid harns, the parts as was stuck to the dory?" asked Daniel, who got there first.

Tom remembered the story of the iron needle swallowed by dogs, and how it had been found.

"Gone," he said shortly.

"We could've sold it!" said Dan'l. "Fer money!" he added.

"Sold it?" said Tom. "Are ya cufferin' me? Who'd buy such a thing? Too tough to eat." He spat again. "An' disgustin'," he added.

"A feller belongs to St. John's," said Daniel. "He's crazy fer such stuff."

Pastor Gabriel was panting hard as he came up. "Oh, no, is it gone?" he said, knuckling the bald spot on the back of his head as was his habit in times of stress. Tom thought the pastor should not rub so hard, as the bald spot seemed to be getting bigger.

"That's all right, Rev'rend," said Theophilous Piccot. "'Twas nice of ya to think on it. No sense frettin' fer what we don't got."

"Well," said Tom, "I did set aside a short bit. I was ordainin' it fer a dock rope."

He reached to the top of the woodpile. And there it was, the pale coiled length of mysterious "kraken."

"You must walk it to St. John's," said the minister, rubbing his bald spot furiously. "You know where the Presbyterian church is, a white cross on top, Devon Row? Go back of it, and you'll find a white house, two-story—"

The tentacle was the slenderest part of the giant squid's arms. Even so it was thick as Tom's wrist, and heavy where he looped the coils around his chest and shoulders for ease of carrying.

Despite the cool October air Tom sweated as he walked the nine miles. He crossed the hills and took the paths and the slightly wider roads until at last he and Murphy stood before a two-story white house, smaller than the merchant's, lacking brick or marble, but substantial, a nice, snug place to live.

Tom knocked. A maidservant answered. "Yis, b'y?" she said.

Inside and just past her, Tom glimpsed high shelves. On

them were books. Not just one or two, but hundreds. He blinked. "I come to see Preacher Harvey. Got me a big squid's harn," said Tom, using the outport name for devil-fish tentacle.

"What fer did ya bring that smelly thing here?" said the maid, wrinkling her nose.

"I was told he pays money fer such," said Tom. All at once he realized how foolish that sounded. As if someone would pay for a piece of dead fish too tough and disgust-ing to eat. He had made the long trip for nothing. He had hoped he might get a penny or a half-cent coin, at least, enough to bring home a handful of sweetness, sugar foo-faraw for the littles. But now—

"What is it, Eileen?" came an educated voice.

"'Tis somebody wi' the harn of yer gert ugly squid, sir—shall I send 'im away?"

"No, no, no! Let him in, let him in!"

Before Tom was halfway through the door, Moses Harvey was on him like a friendly avalanche.

"My boy, my boy, what have you got?" he shouted, clap-ping his hands in delight. He was about fifty years, with short-cropped white hair and wrinkles on his neck, but the face and expression of an excited child. He had deep blue eyes that blinked rapidly.

"Let's unroll it!" he said, yanking out a drawer and for-getting to close it, whipping out a cloth tape measure.

"Out front, if ya doesn't mind, sir!" said the maid, shut-ting the door behind them whether they minded or not.

Fast as Tom could roll out the arm, Moses Harvey raced along it with the tape. He made clucking noises like a bird. Tom watched in amazement.

"Nineteen feet six inches long, more than three times the height of a man! Ha-haaa! At last! At last! My boy, you don't know what this means! With this—" he clutched the tentacle tip, thrust it at Tom— "I hold in my hands the key to a mystery! For the first time the world has proof—positive, undeniable proof! The devilfish, the kraken, the giant squid exists! This is no mythical beast, no tale to frighten children! Do you know, *until this moment* almost no reputable scientist has believed in the kraken, aside from the eminent teuthologist Japetus Steenstrup in the Netherlands, and he—"

"We knowed about squids a long time, sir," said Tom, seeing the man was crazy and wondering if he was dangerous, "we in t' outports. Me grandfather used one to manure the gardens. But I needs to know, do ya want t' offer me somethin' fer this squid harn? 'Cause I ordains it fer a dock rope, s'posin' ya don't."

"Will you take ten shillings?"

"Ten shillin's?" Tom's disbelief was plain. The man was making fun of him. Such a quantity of money! Tom Piccot wasn't a fool. He made an impolite noise and bent down to pick up the tentacle. All that walk for nothing and nine miles more ahead.

Moses Harvey stopped him. "Well, all right then, twenty shillings, one pound, but that's as high as I can go, mind you. I'm in debt to my ears right now."

"Debt?" Tom said, disbelieving the money, picking up on the one part that sounded real. "Oh, we knows about debt! Me father, Theo Piccot from Portugal Cove, he owes a hunnert fourteen pounds an' ten shillin's t' the merchant right now. If we don't pay it tomarrow on settlin'-up day, we'll get neither credit nor yet winter food." He shook his head.

"You're from Portugal Cove?" asked the white-haired gentleman scientist. "What do you want with credit?"

Tom looked at him in disbelief. Didn't this man know anything?

"Fer food, Rev'rend," Tom said, speaking slowly and softly, hoping this crazy man would not get violent. "You know—flour, molasses, salt, hardtack—stuff we needs but can't make fer ourselves?"

"So why don't you sell direct to Bell Island?"

Tom took a cautious step backward, ready to run.

"Nobody lives on Bell Island. Not merchants, nobody."

Then Moses Harvey smiled. For a moment he reminded Tom of another old man who also had blue eyes like windows to the summer sky.

Preacher, gentleman, scientist, the best writer of his country and time—Moses Harvey reached in his pocket. He pulled out some lint, two halfpence, a red handkerchief, and a piece of pink-and-blue paper with Queen Elizabeth's face on one side. He handed the paper to Tom, who studied it, unsure if this was money.

Then Moses Harvey spoke again, more slowly, calmer this time. "You have done me a very great favor, young man. Now I am going to do one for you. Come along with me. There is someone I think you will want to meet."

When Tom went home that night, he and Murphy rode in the coach. Beside him sat Moses Harvey, wanting to find out every detail he could about the giant squid.

And across from them sat a bearded man whom Tom had met once before.

The day of reckoning dawned fresh and clear with a warm wind born in the west. Tom's skin tingled as he waited with the others in the village square; he fairly ached with the excitement of secret knowledge. Today his whole world might change.

Taking advantage of the fine weather, the merchant's

tables were set up outside this time on the flat patch beside the wooden fish-making stages and the landwash on the edge of the sea. The thronelike chairs were already placed, each with a scarlet swansdown cushion ready for merchants' behinds.

The fishermen did not have chairs. They took it for granted they would stand and wait. Strangely, though, all the families were here together, not just a couple at a time.

Tom's news traveled swiftly, and while no one quite believed it, everyone wanted to see what would happen.

The merchant's sailors were out there, too, ready to move fish aboard ship. Tom noticed they carried belaying pins now, the short heavy clubs stuck under their belts. Loading fish would be awkward like that, Tom thought. Why were they carrying clubs?

There was the magistrate in his blue uniform. Tom wondered where he kept the little hammer, the one that was used to tack up the dispossess notice when somebody's house was taken away.

At last the lodge door opened. The merchant, his son, and the servants came out.

As they approached the tables Tom observed his enemy.

Young Edmund Treadwell wore a gray, three-cornered hat above a white-powdered wig. He had on a royal blue coat with gleaming brass buttons—Tom knew who would have polished those buttons—a silk ruffled shirt, and fawn pants, white stockings, and buckled leather shoes.

Tom looked at him and wished for lightning—a great shivering bolt of frying electricity—to strike down his enemy, leaving nothing but ashes and shiny lumps of polished melted brass.

But the sky remained clear. Only a chill twist of wind flexed across the square.

And there beside Edmund was the merchant himself.

Ezekiel Treadwell dressed modestly, shunning outward show of wealth. Clad in black, he was small, very old, but active as a bird. He had nervous, quick movements and thin, dry hands he rubbed together now with a whispering, scouring sound. He was a narrow man with a face all wrinkled and pox-scarred, but cheerful in outward appearance. Folks said he could smile when he took a family's home.

Ezekiel Treadwell smiled and waved so amiably.

Behind the Treadwells came the servants, silently.

Rosie! Tom saw her walking, eyes downcast as she had been so recently taught, five humble steps back of the master. In her hands was a cloth-wrapped iron pot of hot tea, in case Master Edmund required refreshment.

So long, Tom thought, since Rosie went into collar, taking service as a maid. A year? More. The merchant was a week later this year for reasons of his own convenience.

Rosie. She was still beautiful, but he didn't like how she walked so slowly. The skip was gone from her step. For a moment he thought she would not even raise her eyes to look for him. Then she did. Tom flinched. In her eyes was the look of a trapped animal. A person can be caught by money needs just as surely as the lynx they'd trapped last winter. Tom's heart thundered, and he knew he would do whatever it took to get her free.

The clerk showed his master the first name on the list. The ritual began.

"Anderson, James." Merchant Edmund Treadwell's voice was clear and carrying. The put-on English accent seemed to stiffen everyone, calling them all to attention.

"Indebtedness, 103 pounds," intoned the clerk.

"I cedes me place to the Piccots," said skinny James

Anderson the elder, twisting his hat nervously.

"Pardon?" said Ezekiel Treadwell.

"Let the Piccots go first; they has something to say," said James Anderson. Then, surprisingly, he plopped his hat back on his head.

The clerk and the merchant looked at each other. Edmund did nothing, neither smiled nor yawned.

"I have no objection," said Ezekiel Treadwell.

"Piccot, Theophilous," intoned the clerk. "Indebtedness 114 pounds, 10 shillings. Are these your fish?"

"They are," said Theophilous, stepping out from the crowd. He did not take off his cap at all. And though he could barely see them, he looked straight ahead at the merchant and his son.

For ten minutes all was quiet in the square. The culler worked swiftly, lifting and turning each fish from each pile, two sailors beside him, re-stacking the fish. That portion of Theo's fish cured with brine—the poor man's cure—was in separate stacks. The culler stopped when he got to these. He looked at Theo, puzzled at the obvious difference in quality.

"We had to cure them fish wi' brine. Salt runned out," Theo explained.

The culler nodded briefly. When he was done, he went to the Treadwells and whispered to them in tones too low for others to hear.

"I'll handle this one, Father," said Edmund. He slid the clerk's account book before him. He could read and do figures, too.

"Theophilous Piccot offers one hundred quintals of dry weight cod adjudged in quality"—everybody waited—"*nine part West Indies, one part cullage.*" Same as calling their fish trash.

A gasp went through the assembled fishermen. They all knew good fish, and the sun-cured cod of the Piccots was the best: triangular slabs of golden codsteak, scented with spruce boughs, the highest quality food.

Even the culler looked shocked. "Sir?" he said, thinking his judgment had been misheard.

Edmund silenced him, lifting one heavy-ringed hand.

"Me fish is cullage, hey?" said Theo.

Someone sucked in breath. It was not safe to argue with the merchant.

"And West Indies, yes," said Edmund, grinning.

"And how much do ya offer me—fer those miserable fish?"

"Ten pounds, four shillings."

Tom waited for his father to explode at such a ridiculous offer. The Piccots were being stepped on, it was plain. The merchants were making an example of them.

But Theo only said, in a voice that did not tremble, "An' me barrels over there?"

He nodded toward three and a half dozen handcrafted barrels, bound with twine, carefully fit, bonded from the trees Tom and Daniel had chopped and dragged home.

"One pound," Edmund said, leaning forward.

"Fer all of them?"

"Yes."

"An' me credit?" continued Theophilous, dragging it out to the last.

"Denied."

"Well, now, son—" began the elder merchant soothingly.

"Denied!" repeated Edmund, slamming his hand on the table.

"Our credit is still cut off. We barely made it through the year. All our supplies is gone. You would let us starve."

Theo spoke as if he did not understand and wished to have it clear.

Suddenly Tom knew he had to stand beside his father right now. He walked out into the square, heard footsteps behind him and knew who it was. They were all in this together: Ma, Lynny, Baby Sally, Mark Josephus. Daniel Squires, too. They were what this was all about.

"Me family," said Theo.

"You should have labored harder for them," said Edmund. "But he who will not work shall not be fed."

And then he lifted his hands as if to say, what can I do?

An object flew through the air. Tom thought at first someone had thrown a rock, but it traveled too slow and landed heavily beside Edmund's feet. It was an iron pot. The stopper fell out as it landed. Tea splashed and steamed on the cold ground. He yanked his buckled shoes away, lest they be soiled.

Rosie stepped away from the servants. Her hand went to her white linen cap and snatched it off. She looked at it for a moment, at all the grace and style and elegance it represented. She had been living in a wonderful house, eating the very best food, leftovers or not. Fears of starvation had been over for her. But Rosie May Crandall shook out her long auburn hair. She tossed the linen servant's cap down in front of Edmund's feet. "I quits ya, you fat, feathered—pompadoodle!"

"Silence!" snapped Edmund. He had never been spoken to in such fashion. And by a girl, his servant?

"I'll not!" said Rosie. "These are good people. I've a-knowed 'em all me life. And you'm killin' 'em, givin' 'em hardly no pay fer their work. What's next? Will ya take their home away 'cuz they can't pay the debt, seein' as ya won't give 'em a fair price? You'm no man!"

"I'll have you whipped," snarled Edmund, broad face darkening to rage. "Constable, take this—this female in charge. She is in collar to me. I own her contract," snapped Edmund.

The uniformed constable took one step forward. So did Tom. To Rosie's side.

But Rosie was still talking. "Me contract was fer a year and a day, which was up yesterday!" she said. "I hadn' made up me mind yet whether to go on. But I can't work fer such as you. Do yer worst. You owns me no more!" Her chin was out, and she was shaking.

The magistrate looked at Edmund. Edmund looked at his hands for a moment, then to his father.

Now Ezekiel spoke, and the old merchant's smile did not grow less.

"Don't excite yourself, my son. Remember the old proverb? Each dog has his day, *and each bitch, too.*" Tom drew a breath, but Ezekiel went on. "We'll see how bold young Missy talks when her own debt is called in. Perhaps a homeless winter in the snow will cool her temper—and anyone who offers her shelter shall be cut off as well! Oh, and I believe the Widow Crandall is her mother? How unfortunate. Still, the parent is responsible for the child, and it will be good for both to learn the virtue of humility, and obedience to one's betters."

Rosie paled but stood her ground beside the Piccots. Tom moved so that his shoulder was touching hers.

Now Edmund spoke. "But this—wench is right about one thing. Constable, these Piccots owe my father and me a great deal of money. They clearly have neither the means nor the inclination to pay my legal rights. I believe you can see their home, that brown shack on Grayman's Beard Hill over there? Please nail the dispossess notice to their door.

They also own a fish-making stage and two dories, one large, one small. All such property, and anything else they may possess, now belongs to the Treadwell family. I want them searched. To the skin."

The constable scratched his face. He used to have hair on his chin, and every so often it itched where the fisherman's beard had been.

"Hold yer oars a bit, Constable," said Theo. "Don't be gettin' out yer little hammer and them dispossessin' papers. Not just yet."

Theo turned to Rosie. He smiled, like sunlight in a storm. "I won't be fergittin' what ya done this day," he said.

Then his gaze returned to the merchant. The smile faded. He spoke and his voice rumbled. "There is somethin' ye merchant fellers don't know. Or maybe ye does know an' just don't want us to find out. Me son is the one who knowed first, an' 'tis right he should be the one to say it now in front of ever'body."

Tom's knees shook, feeling all eyes turn to him. "They is goin' to be a *mine*, a iron mine, just across the Tickle on Bell Island," he said.

"A child," sneered Ezekiel. "What can he know of men's business?"

"You'm right 'bout that," agreed Tom, glad to get the attention off himself, "but there's a feller here as does know."

The fishermen parted. From the back of the crowd came the tall, bearded man Tom had met yesterday, and once before, when the man had held a lantern in the storm.

Edmund looked at his father, then back.

"Who are you, sir?" asked Edmund.

"I am Captain Josiah Fulton," said the bearded man,

"part owner in the soon-to-be constructed Bell Island mine. My ship is the clipper *Shenandithet*. We had been using gravel from Bell Island for ballast in my ship. But the color of those rocks . . . " He paused. "Iron! I met this young man" —he pointed to Tom— "not long ago, when I was taking metallurgic samples of Bell Island's gravel. Tests confirmed the dirt as high-grade iron ore."

"That's what them jelly jars was fer!" said Ma.

"What do it mean t' us?" someone yelled. "We is fishermen, not miners!"

Tom burst in again. "A hunnert men'll be workin' there, some hired from right here. They got to eat, don't they? That means fish! Oh, sorry, sir."

"Keep going, son. I am sure they would rather hear it from you," said Josiah Fulton.

Tom went on slowly, trying to get it right.

"See, the mine is part-owned by the Americans, folks from the States down there. We'll be sellin' our fish to them, direct. They has money, an' they pays in gold. Me father's barrels over there? Bought an' paid for, and seven dozen more ordered, and part paid for in advance."

His father handed Tom a leather pouch. The contents clinked as Tom raised it high so all could see.

"We none of us has to take nonsense from the Treadwells, niver no more."

Ezekiel Treadwell looked around, then spoke quickly. "I had been saving this for a surprise, but I see the cat is out of the bag."

Tom was puzzled by this. Cat? Bag? He saw neither feline nor sack.

But Ezekiel continued. "Naturally, I have known about this proposed mine for some time, and it may prove to be good news, indeed, as long as we are careful not to plunge too quickly into these uncharted waters. I will be handling the complicated transactions (about which you need not concern yourselves), but it was always my intention you should share in our good fortune.

"My fellow merchants will doubtless chide me for such foolishness, but I am, here and now, doubling the price I will pay for your fish."

A buzz of shocked conversation shot through the crowd. Double?

"As well he might," said Captain Fulton, "since he and the others were planning to sell that same fish to us—at ten times that price again."

Uproar.

"Normally I don't mix in local politics," Josiah Fulton continued, "but if you folks will sell direct to me, I can pay you a great deal more than he does while still saving money myself. It would be good for you and good for me, cut my food expenses way down."

"Talk's nought but wind," said Ezekiel quickly. "We hear a lot of words from you, sir, but what have you got to back it up?"

The Yankee captain took a silver whistle from his pocket and clapped it to his lips. The whistle shrilled. All Portugal Cove seemed to hold its breath.

For a long moment nothing seemed to happen. And then a clipper ship came round Sail Point and headed into the cove.

"On that ship is a safe full of gold," the Captain said.

The fishermen groaned in disbelief.

Theophilous spoke once more. "As fer the Piccots of Portugal Cove, we'll be *payin' you off,* Merchant Treadwell, right now. We're tearin' our page from yer book. Son" — he gestured to Tom— "pay the man."

As in a dream, Tom walked to the merchant. With trembling fingers he emptied the pouch—coins of silver and gold and the one-pound note from Moses Harvey—on the table. The old man's greedy fingers did not hesitate to snatch it all. He counted quickly, nodded.

But when he reached for the leather account book, Theo stopped him.

"No, sir, don't you touch that page," he said. "Me missuz will do it. She is the one that have felt the debt most, always worryin', workin' little miracles iv'ry day, tryin' to keep our little ones alive."

Marian Piccot walked to the desk and reached her hands out to the book.

"Uh, right here, ma'am!" said the clerk, afraid she would tear the wrong place.

Marian ripped the page away quickly but surprisingly did not tear it into shreds. "Write 'paid in full' across it," she said to the clerk, who was too shocked to disobey.

Lynny's friend Peggeen, the schoolteacher, crowded in close to read, making sure the words on the page said exactly what they should. Tom looked in, too, and some words he knew and some words he did not. Words. Words could cheat a people or set them free. He remembered his book about Abraham Lincoln. He had never quite finished it. Now he knew he would.

"I'll be seein' ya in school, Peggeen. I mean Miz Peggeen, ma'am," he said, and she smiled at him.

Ma held up the torn-out page. "We'll be keepin' this," she said, "to remember this day fer always, the day we tore the page an' broke the debt."

"Now," Tom said with a chill in his gut, "there's one more thing." And he looked at the merchant's son.

"What's that?" snapped Edmund.

"They was some ugly words passed a moment ago," said Tom, "'bout dogs. An' bitches. One thing an' another. P'rhaps it was spoke in the heat of the moment. So I'm wonderin' now, *b'y*, if you would care to apologize fer yer father, him being old an' prob'ly not right in the head."

Edmund snorted through his nose. Then he straightened his arms and inhaled deep with satisfaction. "Thank you," he said. "Thank you very much. This has been such a boring day till now."

"Don't be fergittin' yer little black gloves," said Tom.

Rosie spoke quickly under her breath. "Tom, them's cheatin' things!"

Edmund heard. He smiled as he removed both his hat and the powdered white wig. He undid the brass-buttoned coat and set it neatly aside, then began to unbutton his shirt.

"One should practice the art of self-defense," said Edmund. He slipped off his rings lest his knuckles be cut, then tugged on the gloves with the metal ridges bulging the fabric.

"It is called boxing. Have you heard of that, my ignorant little outport peasant?"

"You shimmickin' maneen!" said Tom. "Always talkin' like you got a straw up yer nose! Why do ya pretend to be from England? You was born here same as we. Can't ya not even *talk* like a man?"

"Like you? An uneducated nothing, fit only to associate with the other low scum like yourself?" Edmund spoke slowly and distinctly.

The fishermen stiffened.

"We was good enough to make you rich!" James Anderson said.

"Now, now," said old Ezekiel quickly, spreading his

hands, "let us be calm, not do things we may regret later when the passion of the moment has gone by. The merchant and the fisherman—we're all in this together, are we not? We should *reason* this out, be a happy family once again. These outsiders—people you do not even know. How can you trust them? Surely you remember how the Treadwell family has risked money on the cove time and time again, advancing credit to you. We risked that money, could have lost it!"

"Ye risks yer money," said Theo. "We only risks our lives."

"True an' certain, that it is," said Noddy Weathers, stepping up beside Theophilous. Other voices rumbled agreement; other fishing families crowded in beside the Piccots.

The sailors of the merchant's ship stepped up behind the table. One burly man with a broken nose took out the belaying pin from his belt.

Edmund waved them back with a languid gesture of black-gloved hands. "This is but a moment's . . . entertainment. Unless our little outport boy wishes to change his mind and crawl back into his hole?"

Tom remembered the power of Edmund's punches. "Don't be all day gettin' ready," he said. "I got more important things t' do this day than mess wi' the likes o' you."

"Don't worry," said Edmund, "this won't take long."

Murphy stood up. The dog made no noise, but his eyes were fixed on Tom and the merchant's son before him.

Edmund turned to his father. "That mongrel again, the one I told you about."

A rope was produced. Murphy was tied, and the knot inspected by Edmund's father (for his son's security) and by Tom's father (for the good of the dog). The knot was a bowline; it would neither loosen nor strangle. The rope was a dory's hawser, thick as a man's little finger. Not even

Murphy could break loose now.

On both sides the folks moved back, clearing the square.

Then the merchant spoke again. "This is foolishness. Hot tempers speak words too often regretted later. I am willing to be generous. I will reinstate the Piccots' credit, even overlook the grievous insult to my family. As for the Americans—they are here for an hour, a quick profit, and then gone. They don't care about you. When they leave, you will have nothing. Whom will you turn to then?"

"Anybody but a Treadwell!" someone shouted, and the crowd approved.

"No! Think!" said Ezekiel, eyes glittering. "Use your reason! This hairless boy, his half-blind father—they stand for sudden, radical change, which is dangerous and to be feared. We—my son and I—we are the Treadwell family. We stand for what is *right* and *proper* and *real!*"

It got quiet. "'E's got a point," someone said. "We'd be goin' against the way things is."

Then Peggeen stepped forward once more. "Just because something *is* does not mean it is *right*," she said. "I think it is time for a change."

"I'll take care of this, Father," said Edmund, and he removed his silk shirt. There was a gasp as he handed the shirt to a servant, who looked almost afraid of it, the price of a year's wages in his hands. But the gasp was not for the garment.

Newfoundlanders are not big people, tending more toward wiriness than mass.

Edmund looked different with his shirt off. His chest was great slabs of pectoral muscle; arms and shoulders were heavy as a bear's. His belly was perhaps a trifle thick from much good food and wine, but he swelled his lungs with deep satisfaction, swung back his brawny arms, shook his head to one side, back and forth again. They heard his back go *clicklick* as the vertebrae re-aligned themselves.

Tom took off his sweater, too, but not for display. He figured he might get his shirt ripped and wanted to save Ma the sewing. He looked funny with the shirt of his white longjohns showing. But a ripple of chill wind rushed past them, and Tom was glad for the layer of clothes. He might not look as scary as the other, but he was warmer.

Edmund put his hands up in the English boxing stance. A blue vein showed on the curve of his biceps.

Suddenly the terror left Tom. Now, at last, the waiting was over. He shook out his shoulders, got ready to move.

They circled. Tom noticed how Edmund's chin was protected, tucked behind his left shoulder, and both fists high, also to protect the jaw.

And then Tom remembered the devil of the woods.

"Hey, pretty boy," he said, and made a kissy-kissy noise.

Edmund smiled and came ahead in shuffling short steps. The foot-scraping walk looked mechanical, but it meant readiness to punch.

Tom balanced lightly, right hand by his chest, the left pointed down. His fists were loose, only partly closed.

Edmund slowed a little, studying Tom. Tentatively the larger boy jabbed with the left, an investigative flick not intended to connect. He wanted to find out what would happen. Tom ducked to the side and stepped back. Edmund shuffled forward.

"Don't hurt my brother!" came a high, clear, childish voice.

"It's all right, Baby Sally, we're just playing," said Tom. "Take 'er home, Lynny," he added.

Baby Sally frowned, left eye squinting because of the scar.

"Your sister is amazingly ugly," said Edmund, "or is that

your pet monkey?"

Without Tom's knowledge or consent, his left foot lashed up. His legs opened like a pair of scissors, quick! He felt the shock of impact through his toes. Edmund flew back, holding his face. He took his hand away, astonished. His lower lip was split.

"Foul! I cry foul," he said to the uniformed constable. "Unsportsmanlike conduct to fight with the feet!"

"'E's got a point, b'y," said the constable. "Can't kick a man in the head. Might kill 'im."

"What about them gloves 'e's wearin'?" yelled Theo. "They is weapons sure an' certain!"

The constable rubbed his chin again. "Sir, may I see one of your gloves, please?"

"Never mind," said Edmund, tugging off the gloves and throwing them down. They landed with a soft thud, heavy with the metal strips inside.

"All right, no kicks to the head, now," said the constable to Tom. "Nor to the privates," he added in a lower voice so the ladies wouldn't hear.

Edmund jabbed with his left at Tom's face, followed with a right cross.

Tom stepped to his left, avoiding the blow, then brought his right foot in and up, thumping Edmund hard on the shoulder. He had aimed for the larger man's stomach, but missed, and was blocked by the boxer's reflexes.

Edmund grabbed for Tom's foot, caught hold, lifted and tossed.

Tom lit on his back, came up in a roll.

Edmund charged.

Tom ran.

The sailors laughed, thinking Tom afraid. Edmund stopped and turned to them. "Look at him run!" he said.

Tom turned and kicked Edmund, right where the woodsdevil had bit the bear.

Edmund roared, too, and came after Tom, and his size did not mean he was slow.

But Tom was faster. He gained distance, darting around his own piles of fish ahead of the furious Edmund.

"Come on, fat boy," he yelled, looking back for one mistaken instant. *Bump!* He ran into two grinning sailors blocking his way. To his left and right were stacks of Piccot fish. He *knew* those fish, some as individuals, since they cost so much work. He saw one great big cover fish, skin up to protect the others. That fish had been huge when caught, probably eighty pounds wet. Now of course it was half that or so, split and dried, but still it was a wonderful fish, not *cullage!* The injustice of it raged through him.

"Leave go o' him!" Theo yelled at the sailors. They let go Tom's arms.

"But don't let him run," said Edmund, coming in slow, gloating, ready for the kill.

Tom whirled and grabbed the cover fish, swung it with all his wiry power.

Splat! Edmund staggered. The fish did not break.

"That's cullage fish 'cordin' to you," said Tom, "'cept cullage fish breaks easy!"

Edmund came like a bull. Tom slammed him again, dropped the fish, and jumped left, knocking over part of the pile. Edmund ploughed into the rest.

He came up covered with salt and rage, his face a blaze of red.

"Cullage fish is slimy," explained Tom patiently, "'cause it ain't been cured right, see? But you don't have much slime on yer face, so maybe that fish ain't cullage?"

"Arrrh!" said Edmund, and came ahead, boxing stance

forgotten, hands wide and clutching, big legs lifting, feet crushing good fish.

Tom stood wide-legged, waiting, left side to his attacker. His weight was balanced forward.

Edmund's thick arms reached, the red face neared, teeth bare—and the heavy hands came up like claws.

Tom exploded. Pivoting on his left foot, he slammed his right knee to Edmund's solar plexus, the top of the stomach where the muscular armor of all men is thin. With Edmund's forward momentum, the knee connected with terrific impact. There was a *whoof* of knocked-out breath.

Edmund bent over, yawping helplessly, making little clicking sounds in his throat. Breath knocked out, lungs empty, stomach muscles temporarily paralyzed, he could do nothing else. Standing in the middle of the Piccots' good fish, he appeared to be bowing to Tom, who lowered his hands.

"How do ya like it, bein' helpless?" asked Tom. "That's how we feels, most o' the time, the way ye merchant folk use us. I could hurt ya now, easy," he said, "but I has no wish to do harm t' any man. If ya wants our troubles over now, we can call it a voyage."

A moment passed, two. Edmund found his breath. And lunged.

Tom danced back lightly, but got too proud. Edmund feinted left, Tom ducked to the right—into an upward-climbing heavy right cross, the same blow that had felled him before. This time the punch caught Tom square over the heart. He flew back.

Edmund swarmed him, crowding in to get him before he could run. Throwing reckless punches, he drove Tom back, back, along the shore, on the slippery rocks of the landwash. Tom partly dodged and deflected the punches, but partly he just took them. They did not actually hurt, he was too wound up for that, but each blow numbed him slightly, whittling at his consciousness.

Tom stumbled backward, trying for time to recover before Edmund caught him square with a full-strength punch. Tom stepped on the edge of a wooden board. The footbridge. To Grandfather's island.

Up and onto the footbridge they went, over the drop-off where the water went deep, where the ill-fated fish trap had been. Tom felt his strength and balance returning. Just a couple more seconds and he—

A big fist closed on his chest, grasping the shirt of his longjohns. Tom was stopped and turned, pushed back against the walkway's wood railing.

"Hold still!" said Edmund, as if Tom was going to listen. He had Tom's shirt in his right hand and was thumping with his left, trying to steady Tom's face for the one solid punch that would end it.

Tom wiggled violently side to side, denying the solid connection of fist to face. Edmund changed tactics, grabbed his free hand around Tom's neck and squeezed. His other hand worked up and joined the clutch.

Tom threw a punch across the choking hands, smack into Edmund's nose. Red droplets flew. The heavier man just shook his head and shoved Tom back. Tom tried to punch again, but there seemed to be no power in his hands. He tried to kick, but Edmund was too close. Red mist began before Tom's eyes. His spine felt as if it were breaking, with both struggling men pressed hard on the single handrail.

Tom heard a snap and thought it was his back.

He felt the vacancy of empty air. The handrail had broken. Even as they fell, Edmund turned, trying to regain his balance. There was a *thud,* and—*Wham!* Tom was under-water, choking, gagging. Green lights flashed before his eyes. The jagged shock of icy cold shot beneath his clothes as if he was naked in the near-freezing water. He could not breathe. Down and down.

Lungs locked, Tom clawed his way up toward the light, climbing Edmund like a ladder.

A giant's grip clutched the side of Tom's neck! He tried to break free but was helpless in the viselike clamp. The waterline split. His face broke into air. Any second, he knew, he would be turned and punched. He tried to twist and kick, but couldn't. He felt something sharp scratching down his side. What was that no-good son-of-a-merchant doing now?

Only—Edmund was in *front* of him, floating facedown. A patch of red widened around his hair. He must have hit his head on the way down.

If Edmund was there, who was holding—

"Murphy! Leave go me neck, you'm hurtin' me!"

Murphy wasn't eager to let go, not till he was sure his master was safe.

"It's okay, it's okay," said Tom, fumbling for the big dog's neck. He felt the harsh-torn abrasions under the hair where the dog had half-strangled himself fighting the rope, felt the severed end where someone's knife had slashed.

"I loves ya, b'y," said Tom. Exhausted, he clutched the water dog's back, letting Murphy swim for both of them. It was so cold.

But there was Edmund in the way. Still a problem!

Tom muttered something low, not pleasant. Then he sighed and reached out with his free hand. Turning Edmund's head up to the air took no great effort; the dis-tance to shore was not far.

The merchant's son regained consciousness as his back bumped the rocks of the shallows.

He looked up. Half-stunned eyes met Tom's. For a second Tom thought he was going to fight.

Edmund's eyes focused. He shook his head, shivered, looked at Tom's arm holding him. "Why did you—help me?" he said.

"Blessed if I know," said Tom, and let him drop.

The merchant's sailors helped Edmund get up. Where he went after that Tom neither knew nor cared, so long as it was away from here.

He heard the rush of feet in water, looked up, and there was Rosie, getting her skirts wet wading to him.

And there on the shore shouted Lynny, and Ma, Mark Josephus, Baby Sally, Skipper, Daniel, old George, Noddy Weathers, everybody!

There was so much noise, and joy, and also some embarrassment for Tom. He was not used to being hugged and kissed so much, especially in public.

It did seem kind of natural, though, when Rosie slipped her work-rough hand in his. Their fingertips fit together so nicely. Tom looked at her and Rosie looked back.

And hand in hand, they walked up the hill, into the winds of Newfoundland.

...AND TRUTH CONTENT

◆ ◆ ◆

The *Kraken* is a work of fiction based on fact. The great squid battle of October 26, 1873, for example, is a matter of historical record. Ezekiel Treadwell and son, on the other hand, are "made-up" individuals, though merchant cruelty to fishermen was unfortunately quite real.

Certain factual events in this book have been rearranged in time. The schooner *Pearl's* attack on (and sinking by) a giant squid actually occurred on May 10th, 1874, seven months *after* Tom's encounter. I changed the date for purposes of plot. Similarly, the iron mines of Bell Island opened about twenty years later than shown in these pages. I wanted to close my story with the opening of the mines and a visit from a Yankee sea captain because both meant better days ahead. Yankees and miners had cash, and they paid the fishermen directly, often the first money these folks had ever seen.

But the story is not done; the happy ending is not yet. For Tom Piccot, to me, stands for Newfoundland, and that tiny country's struggle goes on. Once a colony of England, now a province of Canada, Newfoundland's wealth has always been fishing; now the fish are almost gone. The great cod banks have been stripped bare, overfished by foreign nations' vast driftnets and giant factory ships. Newfoundland's own small fishing boats lie idle now, rocking at anchor, with only the sound of the guy ropes straining. This beautiful land is increasingly inhabited by tourists like me, who come to shake our heads and sigh and fall in love: with great grey rocks bursting from green hills; with crystal brooks you can stoop down and safely drink; with whales breaching just offshore and islands of rainbow-beaked puffins; with deep, clean sky blue—reaching forever and the waves so clear you see little white rocks tumbling over on the bottom; with the winds at night rushing and whispering by your window while you snuggle warm in an eiderdown comforter. This is a country with people so honest and gentle the police don't carry guns.

Though the folks who were born here must leave the country to find work, hope remains. If the wisdom of the old-style fishermen—they who always threw little ones back so there would be some next year—if their solid tested knowledge and experience can be combined with modern aquacultural techniques of fish-farming, good times can come again. It will be hard. There must be change if we are to bring about a permanently sustainable yield of fish, not only here, but all across the world-ocean. But I believe with all my heart that a lasting prosperity based on a healthy ocean planet can be built and maintained; not just for the few, the wealthy "merchants" of today, but for everyone, and for always.

The fisherman's son Tom Piccot faced up to the kraken: a twelve-year-old boy against a giant squid with ten arms, gnashing beak, and an overall length estimated at eighty feet. Talk about impossible odds! Anyone in his right mind would have told him he had no chance. But the stubborn Newfoundlander kid did not accept "reality"; he would not listen to the "experts." When his father and his neighbor resigned themselves to die, Tom would not quit. He picked up that little bait ax, and he chopped off those gigantic arms. And they took the squid's arm home with them, instead of the other way around.

May we face our own impossibilities with so much courage, and at the last find our way safely home.

FOR MORE INFORMATION

The classic book on octopuses and squid is *Kingdom of the Octopus* by Frank W. Lane, Sheridan House, New York, 1974, which also contains an historical account of Tom Piccot's encounter with the giant squid. Another fine book is *Octopus and Squid: The Soft Intelligence* by Jacques Cousteau, A & W Publishers/Doubleday, New York, 1973.

The answer to an overfished ocean? Strict antipollution laws and the development of fish-farming, called mariculture or aquaculture. Read *Seafarm: The History of Aquaculture* by Elisabeth Mann Borgese, Harry N. Abrams, Inc., Publishers, New York, 1980. Incredible photographs.

For more on the Newfoundland dog, read *This Is the Newfoundland: The Official Publication of the Newfoundland Club of America,* edited by M. K. Drury, T. F. H. Publications, Inc., 1978; and *The New Complete Newfoundland* by M. Chern, Macmillan Publishing Co., New York, 1975.

On Newfoundland itself, try *The New Founde Land: A Personal Voyage of Discovery* by Farley Mowat, McLelland/Bantam Books, Canada/New York, 1989, a collection by the author of *Never Cry Wolf.*

For a photographic visit to this beautiful place, open any book by Ben Hansen such as *Newfoundland,* Vinland Press, St. John's, Newfoundland, 1987.

A book I wish every library owned is the *Dictionary of Newfoundland English* by Story, Kirwin and Widdowson, Breakwater Books, St. John's, Newfoundland, 1990. Eight hundred pages of stories and information.

Also recommended are A. R. Scammel's *Collected Works*, Harry Cuff Publications, Ltd., St. John's, Newfoundland, 1990; *The Newfoundland Character*, edited by Ryan and Rossiter, Jesperson Press, St. John's, Newfoundland, 1987; *This Marvelous Terrible Place* by Yva Momatiuk and John Eastcott, Camden House, Ontario, 1989; and too many more to list here.

Because it is sometimes hard to find books about Newfoundland, here is the address of the island's largest bookstore: Dicks & Co. Ltd. Bookstore, 320 Water Street, St. John's, Newfoundland, A1C 5K9, Canada.